SIR QUIXOTE OF THE MOORS

VALANCOURT CLASSICS

Sir Quixote of the Moors

BEING SOME ACCOUNT OF AN EPISODE IN THE LIFE OF THE SIEUR DE ROHAINE

by JOHN BUCHAN

Edited with an introduction by
Kate Macdonald

𝕶𝖆𝖓𝖘𝖆𝖘 𝕮𝖎𝖙𝖞:
VALANCOURT BOOKS
2008

Sir Quixote of the Moors by John Buchan
First published in 1895 by T. Fisher Unwin
First Valancourt Books edition 2008

Library of Congress Cataloguing-in-Publication Data

Buchan, John, 1875-1940.
Sir Quixote of the Moors : being some account of an episode in
the life of the Sieur de Rohaine / by John Buchan ; edited with an
introduction by Kate Macdonald. – 1st Valancourt Books ed.
p. cm.
ISBN 1-934555-38-x (alk. paper)
1. French–Scotland–Fiction. 2. Covenanters–Scotland–Fiction.
I. Macdonald, Kate. II. Title.
PR6003.U13S5 2008
823'.912–dc22

2008002712

Design and typography by James D. Jenkins
Published by Valancourt Books
Kansas City, Missouri
http://www.valancourtbooks.com

CONTENTS

INTRODUCTION

Context

WHEN *Sir Quixote of the Moors* was published in October 1895, John Buchan was twenty years old. *Sir Quixote* was his first novel. He was in his first year at the University of Oxford, reading Greats (Classics) at Brasenose College, but was a little older than the other freshmen, having studied for three years already at the University of Glasgow. Over the past eighteen months he had also published six literary essays, in *Macmillan's Magazine* and the *Glasgow University Magazine*, which he would republish as part of his first essay collection, *Scholar Gipsies* (1896).

Buchan had been experimenting with the short story while writing this novel, and *Sir Quixote of the Moors*, his first published work of fiction, could be described as a novella, a serious work part-way between a full-length novel and a short story. Buchan's original title for the book was just *Sir Quixote* (his publisher, T. Fisher Unwin, added the suffix and lengthy subtitle)[1] and it was written in Scotland while Buchan was a student at Glasgow. Shortly after its publication Buchan became a reader for the *avant garde* London publisher John Lane, replacing the poet and essayist Richard Le Gallienne,[2] and thus had the entrée to *fin de siècle* society, becoming acquainted with the literary hothouse of The Bodley Head and *The Yellow Book*. His first short stories demonstrate that Buchan was strongly attracted to this milieu, but only responded to it under his own terms. Buchan's early fiction, like *Sir Quixote*, shows independence of mind, and a resistance to literary fashions that was underpinned by Buchan's own cultural roots. His one failure, from the end of this period, his fourth novel *The Half-Hearted* (1900), did not work because Buchan had stopped, momentarily, using his own voice. It was also his first attempt at a full-length study of anglicised county society in his own time, rather than a Scottish historical novel. Being a rather new incomer to this society, he didn't quite get it right.

Buchan's literary essays (1894-1899) were largely derivative, following Robert Louis Stevenson, and Matthew Arnold before him, by using the motif of the wandering "scholar gypsy" to embellish contrasts between the lives of the city clerk and of the free traveller. *Sir Quixote* is clearly part of this phase of Buchan's writing interests, where he experimented with a rather elitist view of an idealised way of life. Buchan later claimed that, at this stage in his life, he had read hardly anything of Scottish fiction, and only discovered Sir Walter Scott once he had left Scotland for Oxford.[3] While the literary influences on *Sir Quixote* are vague, it is apparent that the novel also incorporates Buchan's deeply-felt interest in Scottish history, particularly its religious troubles. Paradoxically, Buchan had abandoned the more unrealistic aspects of the "scholar gypsy" rationale in his essays by 1900, because he had turned from essays to fiction. His early stories were tales of adventure and moral challenge, modelled on Sir Walter Scott, Stevenson (again), Kipling and H. Rider Haggard. By 1900, when Buchan left Oxford and London at the age of twenty-five for South Africa, he had published four novels, three collections of essays, poems and stories, an edition of the essays of the sixteenth-century philosopher and politician Sir Francis Bacon (which he had edited aged seventeen), and a history of his own college.

Background

This intimidatingly precocious young man was to become a creative powerhouse, and a best-selling novelist. Buchan is now most famous for his hearty outdoor adventures starring Richard Hannay (*The Thirty-Nine Steps*, 1915; *Greenmantle*, 1916; *Mr Standfast*, 1919; *The Three Hostages*, 1924; *The Island of Sheep*, 1936). He was also a master of the historical novel (for instance, *Midwinter*, 1923; *Witch Wood*, 1927; *The Blanket of the Dark*, 1931), and showed that he could tackle a detective novel (*The Three Hostages*), science fiction (*The Gap in the Curtain*, 1932), short stories, in which he excelled (see *The Runagates Club*, 1928) and the comic romp (*John Macnab*, 1925). Buchan's concern to address the

unfrivolous elements of life in his fiction led him to address urban poverty (*Huntingtower*, 1922) and political intrigue (*A Prince
of the Captivity*, 1933), and one of his finest novels, *Sick Heart River*
(1940), was also his last, an examination of cultural identity and
enduring values at the end of a man's life. Classical allusions,
Biblical tags, and moral values were the bedrock of his fiction,
giving an almost invisible gravitas to his irresistible storytelling
style. Although Buchan took several years to develop his tech-
niques, his innate ability to hold the reader and to speed the story
along was clearly present in *Sir Quixote*.

Buchan was the eldest son of a Scottish Presbyterian minister,
and had grown up in lowland Scottish towns and cities, exposed
as a child and teenager to urban poverty in Fife fishing villages
and in Glasgow's deprived Gorbals district: "We were engaged in
a perpetual fight against destitution and suffering."[4] Once Buchan
arrived at Oxford at the age of twenty, he never lived in Scotland
again, despite going on to write considerable amounts of fiction
set in Scotland and with Scottish characters. After university he
read for the Bar in London, and worked for two years in South
Africa after the Boer War as a civil servant. He wrote for *The
Spectator* and other periodicals for a few years, and then became
a publisher with the Scottish firm Thomas Nelson & Sons. After
his marriage to Susan Grosvenor in 1907, a cousin of the Duke
of Westminster, the young Buchan family (he and Susan were
to have a daughter and three sons) lived in London and later in
Oxfordshire. Buchan served in the First World War as a journal-
ist, a historian and Director of Information for the British government, and, after the war, was a director and Deputy-Chairman of
Reuters and a Member of Parliament. In 1935 he was appointed
governor-general of Canada, and created Lord Tweedsmuir of
Elsfield. As a much-loved figure in Canada, Buchan spent the last
five years of his life there, travelling extensively, and working to
develop Canadian cultural identity. In 1940 he suffered a brain
hæmorrhage while shaving, and never recovered consciousness.
He was sixty five. He had suffered ill-health for half his life, exac-
erbated by overwork during the First World War and a punishing
schedule that he had followed since his Oxford days.

John Buchan was politically and socially ambitious. Through his serial professions and his marriage he acquired a very wide set of influential relations, friends, and acquaintances. He delighted in being able to help or to know someone who could, and he relished how influence could move mountains. He employed this characteristic in his Richard Hannay novels without hesitation, which now reads as a symptom of social networking criticised more for its snobbery than for its utility. Buchan was also ambitious for his books, in that he was very confident of his literary abilities and he knew what he wanted to achieve with them. *Sir Quixote* is a young man's book, but it is not an obvious first novel. It was experimental, tackling a philosophical point in a historical and geographical setting that Buchan knew well from experience.

He intended this novel to be "an effort to show what would be the course of a certain type of character in certain difficult circumstances, and [...] to trace the influence of scene and weather on the action and nature of man."[5] Written shortly after the novel was published, this rather earnest avowal, from a Victorian twenty-year-old who may well have observed Life in the Gorbals and Art at London literary parties, but whose experience was still necessarily limited, supports a much later assessment of *Sir Quixote* as sharing the characteristics of the fiction of Henry James.[6] This is also suggested by Buchan's later memories of that time in his life: "In my undergraduate days I had tried my hand at historical novels, and had then some ambition to write fiction in the grand manner, by interpreting and clarifying a large piece of life."[7] Buchan was never again to write such a "theoretical" text, in the sense of deliberately setting himself a philosophical problem and attempting to explore it in a fictional form.

Sir Quixote is probably the least reissued of all Buchan's novels. It has appeared in only four editions (1895 UK, 1895 USA, 1918 UK, and 1924 UK), because Buchan regarded the novel as a juvenile effort, and told his publisher in 1918 that he did not want it to be reprinted.[8] T. Fisher Unwin went on to reprint the novel in any case, in 1924. Their commercial confidence in Buchan's first, and fairly unknown novel, and Buchan's own reservations about its reissue, were probably influenced by Buchan's new position as a best-selling author. In 1918 he was also a figure of importance working for the British war government. After the war Buchan was to plunge into a new phase of creativity from a position of magisterial authority, in which, from his point of view, his earliest novel, published almost twenty years earlier, was best forgotten. Fisher Unwin clearly felt differently, and expected money to be made from it.

However, it is not clear why Buchan should have wanted to forget about *Sir Quixote*. He did not mention it at all in his autobiography: his crowded life had squeezed the beginnings of his literary career into oblivion. He had no disdain in general for his juvenilia, and always liked his second novel, *John Burnet of Barns* (1898), which shared the subject and setting of *Sir Quixote*. He seems to have liked *Sir Quixote*'s principal character, since the eponymous hero of *John Burnet of Barns* meets and admires the hero of *Sir Quixote* in Leyden. This reuse of a character is an early example of Buchan's use of social wallpaper, of creating a background cast of named but two-dimensional persons to populate the social gatherings of his fiction. However, it was atypical of Buchan to reuse his historical characters, which he afterwards kept quite separate from each other. It may be that although Buchan enjoyed the effect of continuity that a reused character engendered, he did not feel it to be necessary in his historical fiction, whereas in the fiction he wrote set in his own time it seemed to work admirably as a descriptive device.

Buchan's attempt at a Jamesian approach to character may have failed his own expectations. He wrote to the book's dedicatee, his former tutor in Greek at Glasgow, Professor Gilbert Murray, "Now that I have read it in print I don't feel at all satisfied with it. Some of it I like but in a good deal of it I think I have been quite unsuccessful."[9] This uncertainty may also have been reflected in the novel's "American" ending (but see Afterword on page 81 for a discussion of the two endings, and who wrote them.)

Setting

Sir Quixote is intriguingly original, as well as being firmly set in a Scottish tradition of writing about bad weather and tragedy. It appeared in the same year as, for example, Thomas Hardy's *Jude the Obscure* and H.G. Wells's *The Time Machine*, Marie Corelli's *The Sorrows of Satan* and Stephen Crane's *The Red Badge of Courage*. It was also the year of Oscar Wilde's *The Importance of Being Earnest* and *An Ideal Husband*, and Kipling's *The Second Jungle Book*, but none of these works seem immediately connectable with what Buchan was writing about: dreich weather and a man's honour in the face of mindless religious persecution over two hundred years earlier. In Buchan's immediate cultural environment, Robert Louis Stevenson was at the end of his life (he died in December 1894), leaving his bleak and unfinished novel *Weir of Hermiston* to be published in 1896. *Sir Quixote* shares elements of Stevenson's outlook, in that he and Buchan make the wet and coldness of Scottish weather a fundamental part of their plots. In Stevenson's *Kidnapped* and *Catriona*, his hero David Balfour travels rough in poor weather and is thwarted by its vagaries to the risk of his enterprises. Buchan went on to use foul weather in a depressingly unromantic sense in his third novel *A Lost Lady of Old Years* (1899), and it is a constant feature of his contemporary fiction, where the heroes prove their mettle by not only resisting but almost enjoying the challenge of the wet and the cold.

The topography and historical settings of the novels of Stevenson, Buchan, and, above all, Sir Walter Scott, are also significant in determining what Buchan was doing with *Sir Quixote*. Along with Neil Munro, these writers defined the condition of the Scottish historical romance at the end of the nineteenth century, with an output dating from Scott's invention of the genre in the early nineteenth century with *Waverley* (1814). All four writers focused many of their historical novels on the 1745 Jacobite Rebellion and its aftermath, but Buchan was unusual in going further back in time, to address a more fundamental cause for religious, national, and cultural division in Scotland: to the 1680s, the "Killing Times" of the Covenanting period that were a bloody hangover from the Scottish and English Civil Wars of the mid-seventeenth century. He used the Scottish seventeenth century several times in his historical writing and in his historical fiction: *Sir Quixote* was his first attempt to inhabit that space and time.

At the death of Charles II, his Roman Catholic brother James II ascended the throne as King of England and Scotland in 1685, but the rigidly Protestant Covenanting party in Scotland had not stopped their demands for a Protestant state and a Presbyterian rule. The government dragoons hunted down recalcitrant Protestants throughout Scotland, wherever dissent was most widespread, and also in areas of England. Field preachers and those who attended their "conventicles" received the worst persecution. These clergy adhered to the strict doctrine of Calvinistic theocracy and rejected any form of state control or authority over the church, arguing that it should be the church who had a controlling say in the doings of the state. Banned from their usual pulpits, these preachers began taking their sermons and services to the fields and open spaces where the people could follow them. Once widespread persecution had begun, large communities of these preachers and their followers collected together as outlaws; villages and towns were emptied of their male population, either through flight or by being taken by government forces. Although it was regarded later as a tragically unjust period in Scottish history, labelled the "Killing Times" by the contemporary historian Robert Wodrow, according to modern scholarship fewer Covenanting "martyrs" died in the 1680s, for example, than did English nonconformists in English prisons in the same period, or, for that matter, "witches" burned during the Restoration period.[10] It was an undeniably violent period of British history, one of the recurring episodes of domestic religious fundamentalism that has blighted Britain for centuries.

By focusing on this internally controversial aspect of Scottish history in his novel Buchan was inviting comment. His hero would have been expected, in a conventional historical novel, to provide observations and explain to the reader the different points of view which made up the situation, social, political, and otherwise. The historical novel is also expected to be an illustration of the period in which it is set. Buchan subverts the by then conventional device of having a hero at the tail-end of a great event of history, as a commentator and participant, by having his hero reject the part that he could have played (harrying Scots peasants with Kennedy), to ride off into the unknown to find the same black and white situation elsewhere, in a situation where he must decide for himself what is right and wrong. Buchan's message was that it is not possible to evade the responsibility of having an opinion on these deep religious and political matters, and that although de Rohaine rejected Kennedy's choice and methods, he had still to find a workable solution to his own immediate problems.

The story

Buchan's principal concern with *Sir Quixote* was to take apart the faults and excesses of the Covenanters and their cant to reveal a venal struggle for power, hidden under a violent religious fanaticism that had long since lost sight of the message of mercy and love from the New Testament. Faceless forces represent government and the army, but the impersonal and undiscriminating evil of religious fanaticism also seen here would go on to be an important element in Buchan, particularly in his later novels *Salute to Adventurers* (1915) and *Witch Wood* (1927). His hero, de Rohaine, is the antithesis of the people he meets; in religion (he is a lightly-worn Roman Catholic rather than a fervently evangelical Protestant), class (a minor lord, rather than the local minister), standards of living (he is surprised by how good Scotland's food and drink could be), language (he claims to have learned Scots, but can really only converse in a Frenchified English: both good camouflage tricks for a teenage novelist hoping to hide his deficiencies in dialogue), and culture (southern, not northern, and always influenced by religious differences). This isolation enhances the reader's empathy with the hero, while also distancing him from a modern view, since he clearly has opinions we cannot adopt for our own.

Buchan's choice of a middle-aged Frenchman, contemporary with Spinoza, as a hero, lost in a barely post-medieval Scotland, suggests very strongly the idea of a stranger in a strange land. However, the idea is inverted: the strange land is Buchan's own land, even though the times are strange to us. The stranger's own impressions of that land, which are intended to convey an objective report to the reader, tell the story as a narrative of discovery, of himself, and of this land of brutality and foul weather. The hero's feelings and personality create the pivotal crisis of the plot, and in this, as well as the motif of the stranger, Buchan was anticipating his most famous novel, at this point still twenty years in the future. *The Thirty-Nine Steps* (1915) would also share the stranger as a hero, only Richard Hannay would be a twentieth-century South African, and his actions and experiences would form the plot: in no sense can the Sieur de Rohaine or Richard Hannay be described as passengers in those novels. In *Sir Quixote* Buchan was exploring a plot structure which could be reworked and reused.

The plot finally lays its focus on Anne, the daughter of the minister, and an unawakened girl, willing to be taught, to take the hero's impress. As Buchan was barely twenty, it may be assumed that he was describing the relationship between older man and young girl in theoretical terms only. Since he was clearly writing this novel as a philosophical exercise in character analysis (or so he would have liked us to think), two dimensions were enough for Anne, and that is all she receives. It is significant that she has no interests of her own: "she played no chess [...] reading she cared little for, and but for her embroidery work I know not what she would have set her hand to."[11] She is not even given the dignity of a surname. Although Anne is ostensibly an engaged woman, Buchan ensures that she does not refer at all to her fiancé, the fanatic who has gone off to hide on the moors leaving Anne under the protection of de Rohaine. The only natural feelings or direction that Anne has are wholly domestic, under the influence of her father and with no horizon further than her own home. Once de Rohaine, the alien influence and foreign body is introduced to this enclosed environment, Anne begins to change under the outside influence, and the plot is set in motion at last.

Sir Quixote is carefully underplayed and contains no extraneous material to confuse the story's unfolding. It is slight but definite, and although it does not resemble most of Buchan's writing, it has clear links with later works such as *A Lost Lady of Old Years* (1899) and *Midwinter* (1923), which, like *Sir Quixote*, would have been picaresque adventures had Buchan not included the tragedy of thwarted human love to complicate his characters' lives. It is worth noting that, as with his second novel, *John Burnet of Barns*, Buchan's first two heroes were both called John, and they told their stories in the first person. A "Quixote" was, for Buchan, an adventurer to admire, someone to look up to.[12] As a first novel *Sir Quixote* did well to embrace the philosophical problem Buchan wanted to address, but he could not keep himself out of it completely. He used the novel to work out his own religious doubts and resentments (in all his later work there is scarcely one positive portrait of a churchman: they are either fanatics or fools), while maintaining the power the truth of religious belief itself. He quarrelled with dogma and the dogmatic, and in *Sir Quixote* he gave possibly his most passionate denunciation of religious bigotry.

KATE MACDONALD
Ghent

December 24, 2007

KATE MACDONALD is a lecturer in British literature and culture in the Department of English, University of Ghent, Belgium. She is the author of *John Buchan: A Companion to the Mystery Fiction* (2008), and a former editor of the *John Buchan Journal*.

NOTES

1 Andrew Lownie, *John Buchan. The Presbyterian Cavalier.* London: Constable, 1995, 36.

2 Peter MacDonald, *British Literary Culture and Publishing Practice, 1880-1914.* Cambridge: Cambridge University Press, 1997, p. 76.

3 John Buchan, *Memory Hold-the-Door.* London: Hodder & Stoughton, 1940, 81. This may be disingenuous: Buchan's autobiography was selective.

4 Ibid., 40.

5 John Buchan, "Sir Quixote," in *Good Reading About Many Books.* London: T. Fisher Unwin, 291-294, 294.

6 David Daniell, *The Interpreter's House. A Critical Assessment of the Work of John Buchan.* London: Nelson, 1975, 18.

7 John Buchan, *Memory Hold-the-Door.* London: Hodder & Stoughton, 1940, 194

8 Edinburgh University Library Special Collections, Thomas Nelson archive, Gen 1728, B/8/4: letter from John Buchan to George Brown, 7 January 1918.

9 Andrew Lownie, *John Buchan. The Presbyterian Cavalier.* London: Constable, 1995, 35.

10 Michael Lynch, *Scotland. A New History,* London: Pimlico, 1991, 295.

11 John Buchan, *Sir Quixote of the Moors.* Chicago: Valancourt Books, 2008, 48.

12 John Buchan, *Memory Hold-the-Door.* London: Hodder & Stoughton, 1940, 53, 55.

Sir Quixote of the Moors

PREFACE.

THE narrative, now for the first time presented to the world, was written by the Sieur de Rohaine to while away the time during the long and painful captivity, borne with heroic resolution, which preceded his death. He chose the English tongue, in which he was extraordinarily proficient, for two reasons: first, as an exercise in the language; second, because he desired to keep the passages here recorded from the knowledge of certain of his kinsfolk in France. Few changes have been made in his work. Now and then an English idiom has been substituted for a French; certain tortuous expressions have been emended; and in general the portions in the Scots dialect have been re-written, since the author's knowledge of this manner of speech seems scarcely to have been so great as he himself thought.

ON THE HIGH MOORS.

BEFORE me stretched a black heath, over which the mist blew in gusts, and through whose midst the road crept like an adder. Great storm-marked hills flanked me on either side, and since I set out I had seen their harsh outline against a thick sky, until I longed for flat ground to rest my sight upon. The way was damp, and the soft mountain gravel sank under my horse's feet; and ever and anon my legs were splashed by the water from some pool which the rain had left. Shrill mountain birds flew around, and sent their cries through the cold air. Sometimes the fog would lift for a moment from the face of the land and show me a hilltop or the leaden glimmer of a loch, but nothing more—no green field or homestead; only a barren and accursed desert.

Neither horse nor man was in any spirit. My back ached, and I shivered in my sodden garments, while my eyes were dim from gazing on flying clouds. The poor beast stumbled often, for he had travelled far on little fodder, and a hill-road was a new thing in his experience. Saladin I called him, for I had fancied that there was something Turkish about his black face, with the heavy turbanlike band above his forehead, in my old fortunate days when I bought him. He was a fine horse of the Normandy breed, and had carried me on many a wild journey, though on none so forlorn as this.

But to speak of myself. I am Jean de Rohaine, at your service; Sieur de Rohaine in the province of Touraine—a

gentleman, I trust, though one in a sorry plight. And how
I came to be in the wild highlands of the place called
Galloway, in the bare kingdom of Scotland, I must haste to
tell. In the old days, when I had lived as became my rank in
my native land, I had met a Scot—one Kennedy by name—
a great man in his own country, with whom I struck up
an intimate friendship. He and I were as brothers, and he
swore that if I came to visit him in his own home he would
see to it that I should have of the best. I thanked him at the
time for his bidding, but thought little more of it.

Now, by ill fortune, the time came when, what with gam-
ing and pleasuring, I was a beggared man, and I bethought
me of the Scot's offer. I had liked the man well, and I considered how it would be no ill thing to abide in that country
till I should find some means of bettering my affairs. So I
took ship and came to the town of Ayr, from which 'twas
but a day's ride to the house of my friend. 'Twas in mid-
summer when I landed, and the place looked not so bare
as I had feared, as I rode along between green meadows
to my destination. There I found Quentin Kennedy, somewhat grown old and more full in flesh than I remembered
him in the past. He had been a tall, black-avised man when
I first knew him; now he was grizzled—whether from hard
living or the harshness of northern weather I know not—
and heavier than a man of action is wont to be. He greeted
me most hospitably, putting his house at my bidding, and
swearing that I should abide and keep him company and go
no more back to the South.

So for near a month I stayed there, and such a time of
riot and hilarity I scarce remember. *Mon Dieu*, but the feasting and the sporting would have rejoiced the hearts of my
comrades of the Rue Margot. I had already learned much of
the Scots tongue at the college in Paris, where every second
man hails from this land, and now I was soon perfect in it,

speaking it all but as well as my host. 'Tis a gift I have, for I well remember how, when I consorted for some months in the low countries with an Italian of Milan, I picked up a fair knowledge of his speech. So now I found myself in the midst of men of spirit, and a rare life we led. The gentlemen of the place would come much about the house, and I promise you 'twas not seldom we saw the morning in as we sat at wine. There was, too, the greatest sport at coursing and hunting the deer in Kennedy's lands by the Water of Doon.

Yet there was that I liked not among the fellows who came thither,—nay, even in my friend himself. We have a proverb in France that the devil when he spoils a German in the making turns him into a Scot, and for certain there was much boorishness among them, which to my mind sits ill on gentlemen. They would jest at one another till I thought that in a twinkling swords would be out, and lo! I soon found that 'twas but done for sport, and with no evil intent. They were clownish in their understanding, little recking of the feelings of a man of honour, but quick to grow fierce on some tittle of provocation which another would scarce notice. Indeed, 'tis my belief that one of this nation is best in his youth, for Kennedy, whom I well remembered as a man of courage and breeding, had grown grosser and more sottish with his years, till I was fain to ask where was my friend of the past.

And now I come to that which brought on my departure and my misfortunes. 'Twas one night as I returned weary from riding after a stag in the haugh by the river, that Quentin cried hastily as I entered that now he had found something worthy of my attention.

"To-morrow, Jock," says he, "you will see sport. There has been some cursed commotion among the folk of the hills, and I am out the morrow to redd the marches. You shall have a troop of horse and ride with me, and, God's death, we will have a taste of better work."

I cried out that I could have asked for naught better, and, indeed, I was overjoyed that the hard drinking and idleness were at an end, and that the rigours of warfare lay before me. For I am a soldier by birth and by profession, and I love the jingle of steel and the rush of battle.

So, on the morrow, I rode to the mountains with a score of dragoons behind me, glad and hopeful. *Diable!* How shall I tell my disappointment? The first day I had seen all— and more than I wished. We fought, not with men like our-selves, but with women and children and unarmed yokels, and butchered like Cossacks more than Christians. I grew sick of the work, and would have none of it, but led my men to the rendezvous sullenly and hot at heart. 'Twas well the night was late when we arrived, else I should have met with Kennedy there and then, and God knows what might have happened.

The next day, in a great fit of loathing, I followed my host again, hoping that the worst was over, and that hence-forth I should have something more to my stomach. But little I knew of the men with whom I journeyed. There was a cottage there, a shepherd's house, and God! they burned it down, and the man they shot before his wife and chil-dren, speaking naught to him but foul-mouthed reproaches and jabber about some creed which was strange to me. I could not prevent it, though 'twas all that I could do to keep myself from a mad attack.

I rode up to Quentin Kennedy.

"Sir," I said, "I have had great kindness at your hands, but you and I must part. I see that we are made of different stuff. I can endure war, but not massacre."

He laughed at my scruples, incredulous of my purpose, until at last he saw that I was fixed in my determination.

Then he spoke half-kindly:

"This is a small matter to stand between me and thee. I am a servant of the king, and but do my duty. I little thought to have disloyalty preached from your lips; but bide with me, and I promise that you shall see no more of it."

But my anger was too great, and I would have none of him. Then—and now I marvel at the man's forbearance—he offered me money to recompense me for my trouble. 'Twas honestly meant, and oft have I regretted my action, but to me in my fury it seemed but an added insult.

"Nay," said I angrily; "I take no payment from butchers. I am a gentleman, if a poor one."

At this he flushed wrathfully, and I thought for an instant that he would have drawn on me; but he refrained, and I rode off alone among the moors. I knew naught of the land, and I must have taken the wrong way, for noon found me hopelessly mazed among a tangle of rocks and hills and peat-mosses. Verily, Quentin Kennedy had taken the best revenge by suffering me to follow my own leading.

In the early hours of my journey my head was in such a whirl of wrath and dismay, that I had little power to think settled thoughts. I was in a desperate confusion, half angry at my own haste, and half bitter at the coldness of a friend who would permit a stranger to ride off alone with scarce a word of regret. When I have thought the matter out in after days, I have been as perplexed as ever; yet it still seems to me, though I know not how, that I acted as any man of honour and heart would approve. Still this thought was little present to me in my discomfort, as I plashed through the sodden turf.

I had breakfasted at Kennedy's house of Dunpeel in the early morning, and, since I had no provision of any sort with me, 'twas not long ere the biting of hunger began to set in. My race is a hardy stock, used to much hardships and

rough fare, but in this inclement land my heart failed me
wholly, and I grew sick and giddy, what with the famishing
and the cold rain. For, though 'twas late August, the month
of harvest and fruit-time in my own fair land, it seemed
more like winter. The gusts of sharp wind came driving
out of the mist and pierced me to the very marrow. So
chill were they that my garments were of no avail to avert
them; being, indeed, of the thinnest, and cut according to
the fashion of fine cloth for summer wear at the shows and
gallantries of the town. A pretty change, thought I, from
the gardens of Versailles and the trim streets of Paris to
this surly land; and sad it was to see my cloak, meant for no
rougher breeze than the gentle South, tossed and scattered
by a grim wind.

I have marked it often, and here I proved its truth, that
man's thoughts turn always to the opposites of his present state. Here was I, set in the most uncharitable land
on earth; and yet ever before my eyes would come brief
visions of the gay country which I had forsaken. In a gap
of hill I fancied that I descried a level distance with sunny
vineyards and rich orchards, to which I must surely come
if I but hastened. When I stooped to drink at a stream, I
fancied ere I drank it that the water would taste like the
Bordeaux I was wont to drink at the little hostelry in the
Rue Margot; and when the tasteless liquid once entered my
mouth, the disenchantment was severe. I met one peasant,
an old man bent with toil, coarse-featured, yet not without
some gleams of kindness, and I could not refrain from ad-
dressing him in my native tongue. For though I could make
some shape at his barbarous patois, in my present distress
it came but uneasily from my lips. He stared at me stupidly,
and when I repeated the question in the English, he made
some unintelligible reply, and stumbled onward in his way.
I watched his poor figure as he walked. Such, thought I, are

the *canaille* of the land, and 'tis little wonder if their bodies be mis-shapen and their minds dull, for an archangel would become a boor if he dwelt here for any space of time.

But enough of such dreams, and God knows no man had ever less cause for dreaming. Where was I to go, and what might my purpose be in this wilderness which men call the world? An empty belly and a wet skin do not tend to sedate thinking, so small wonder if I saw little ahead. I was making for the end of the earth, caring little in what direction, weary and sick of heart, with sharp anger at the past and never a hope for the morrow.

Yet, even in my direst days, I have ever found some grain of expectation to console me. I had five crowns in my purse; little enough, but sufficient to win me a dinner and a bed at some cheap hostelry. So all through the gray afternoon I looked sharply for a house, mistaking every monstrous boulder for a gable-end. I cheered my heart with think-ing of dainties to be looked for; a dish of boiled fish, or a piece of mutton from one of the wild-faced sheep which bounded ever and anon across my path. Nay, I was in no mood to be fastidious. I would e'en be content with a poor fare, provided always I could succeed in swallowing it, for my desire soon became less for the attainment of a pleasure than for the alleviation of a discomfort. For I was ravenous as a hawk, and had it in my heart more than once to dis-mount and seek for the sparse hill-berries.

And, indeed, this was like to have been my predicament, for the day grew late and I came no nearer a human dwell-ing. The valley in which I rode grew wider, about to open, as I thought, into the dale of a river. The hills, from rising steeply by the wayside, were withdrawn to the distance of maybe a mile, where they lifted their faces through the net-work of the mist. All the land between them, save a strip where the road lay, was filled with a black marsh, where moor birds made a most dreary wailing. It minded me of the cries of the innocents whom King Herod slew, as I had seen the deed represented outside the village church of Rohaine in my far-away homeland. My heart grew sore with longing. I had bartered my native country for the most dismal on earth, and all for nothing. Madman that I was, were it not better to be a beggar in France than a horse-captain in any other place? I cursed my folly sorely, as each fresh blast sent a shiver through my body. Nor was my horse in any better state—Saladin, whom I had seen gaily decked at a procession with ribands and pretty favours, who had carried me so often and so far, who had always fared on the best. The poor beast was in a woful plight, with his pasterns bleeding from the rough stones and his head bent with weariness. Verily, I pitied him more than myself, and if I had had a crust we should have shared it.

The night came in, black as a draw-well and stormy as the Day of Doom. I had now no little trouble in picking out the way from among the treacherous morasses. Of a sudden my horse would have a forefoot in a pool of black peat-water, from which I would scarce, by much pulling, recover him. A sharp jag of stone in the way would all but bring him to his knees. So we dragged wearily along, scarce fearing, caring, hoping for anything in this world or another.

It was, I judge, an hour after nightfall, about nine of the clock, when I fancied that some glimmer shot through the thick darkness. I could have clapped my hands for joy had I been able; but alas! these were so stiff, that clapping was as far from me as from a man with the palsy.

"Courage!" said I, "courage, Saladin! There is yet hope for us!"

The poor animal seemed to share in my expectations. He carried me quicker forward, so that soon the feeble

gleam had grown to a broad light. Inn or dwelling, thought
I, there I stay, for I will go not a foot further for man or
devil. My sword must e'en be my *fourrier* to get me a night's
lodging. Then I saw the house, a low, dark place, unillu-
mined save for that front window which shone as an invita-
tion to travellers. In a minute I was at the threshold. There,
in truth, was the sign napping above the lintel. 'Twas an inn
at length, and my heart leapt out in gratitude.

II.

I FARE BADLY INDOORS.

I DROPPED wearily from my horse and stumbled forward to the door. 'Twas close shut, but rays of light came through the chinks at the foot, and the great light in the further window lit up the ground for some yards. I knocked loudly with my sword-hilt. Stillness seemed to reign within, save that from some distant room a faint sound of men's voices was brought. A most savoury smell stole out to the raw air and revived my hunger with hopes of supper.

Again I knocked, this time rudely and the door rattled on its hinges. This brought some signs of life from within. I could hear a foot on the stone floor of a passage, a bustling as of many folk running hither and thither, and a great barking of a sheep-dog. Of a sudden the door was flung open, a warm blaze of light rushed forth, and I stood blinking before the master of the house.

He was a tall grizzled man of maybe fifty years, thin, with a stoop in his back that all hill-folk have, and a face brown with sun and wind. I judged him fifty, but he may have been younger by ten years, for in that desert men age the speedier. His dress was dirty and ragged in many places, and in one hand he carried a pistol, which he held before him as if for protection. He stared at me for a second.

"Wha are ye that comes dirlin' here on sic a nicht?" said he, and I give his speech as I remember it. As he uttered the words, he looked me keenly in the face, and I felt his thin, cold glance piercing to the roots of my thoughts. I liked

the man ill, for, what with his lean figure and sour counte-
nance, he was far different from the jovial, well-groomed
fellows who will give you greeting at any wayside inn from
Calais to Bordeaux.

"You ask a strange question, and one little needing answer. If a man has wandered for hours in bog-holes, he
will be in no mind to stand chaffering at inn doors. I seek a
night's lodging for my horse and myself."

"It's little we can give you, for it's a bare, sinfu' land,"
said he, "but such as I ha'e ye're welcome to. Bide a minute,
and I'll bring a licht to tak' ye to the stable."

He was gone down the passage for a few seconds, and
returned with a rushlight encased against the wind in a
wicker covering. The storm made it flicker and flare till it
sent dancing shadows over the dark walls of the house. The
stable lay round by the backend, and thither poor Saladin
and his master stumbled over a most villainous rough
ground. The place, when found, was no great thing to
boast of—a cold shed, damp with rain, with blaffs of wind
wheezing through it; and I was grieved to think of my
horse's nightly comfort. The host snatched from a rack a
truss of hay, which by its smell was old enough, and tossed
it into the manger. "There ye are, and it's mair than mony a
Christian gets in thae weary days."

Then he led the way back into the house. We entered
a draughty passage, with a window at one end, broken in
part, through which streamed the cold air. A turn brought
me into a little square room, where a fire flickered and a
low lamp burned on the table. 'Twas so home-like and
peaceful that my heart went out to it, and I thanked my
fate for the comfortable lodging I had chanced on. Mine
host stirred the blaze and bade me strip off my wet garments. He fetched me an armful of rough homespuns, but
I cared little to put them on, so I e'en sat in my shirt and

waited on the drying of my coat. My mother's portrait, the one by Grizot, which I have had set in gold and wear always near my heart, dangled to my lap, and I took this for an evil omen. I returned it quick to its place, the more so because I saw the landlord's lantern-jaw close at the sight, and his cold eyes twinkle. Had I been wise, too, I would have stripped my rings from my fingers ere I began this ill-boding travel, for it does not behove a gentleman to be sojourning among beggars with gold about him.

"Have ye come far the day?" the man asked in his harsh voice. "Ye're gey-like splashed wi' dirt, so I jalouse ye cam ower the *Angel's Ladder.*"

"Angel's ladder!" quoth I, "devil's ladder I call it! for a more blackguardly place I have not clapped eyes on since I first mounted horse."

"*Angel's Ladder* they call it," said the man, to all appearance never heeding my words, "for there, mony a year syne, an holy man of God, one Ebenezer Clavershaws, preached to a goodly gathering on the shining ladder seen by the patriarch Jacob at Bethel, which extended from earth to heaven. 'Twas a rich discourse, and I have it still in my mind."

"'Twas more likely to have been a way to the Evil One for me. Had I but gone a further step many a time, I should have been giving my account ere this to my Maker. But a truce to this talk. 'Twas not to listen to such that I came here; let me have supper, the best you have, and a bottle of whatever wine you keep in this accursed place. Burgundy is my choice."

"Young man," the fellow said gravely, looking at me with his unpleasing eyes, "you are one who loves the meat that perisheth rather than the unsearchable riches of God's grace. O, be warned while yet there is time. You know not the delights of gladsome communion wi' Him, which makes the moss-hags and heather-busses more fair than the roses of Sharon or the balmy plains of Gilead. O, be wise and turn, for now is the accepted time, now is the day of salvation!"

Sacré what madman have I fallen in with, thought I, who talks in this fashion. I had heard of the wild deeds of those in our own land who call themselves Huguenots, and I was not altogether without fear. But my appetite was keen, and my blood was never of the coolest.

"Peace with your nonsense, sirrah," I said sternly: "what man are you who come and prate before your guests, instead of fetching their supper? Let me have mine at once, and no more of your Scripture."

As I spoke, I looked him angrily in the face, and my bearing must have had some effect upon him, for he turned suddenly and passed out.

A wench appeared, a comely slip of a girl, with eyes somewhat dazed and timorous, and set the table with viands. There was a moor-fowl, well-roasted and tasty to the palate, a cut of salted beef, and for wine, a bottle of French claret of excellent quality. 'Twas so much in excess of my expectation, that I straightway fell into a good humour, and the black cloud of dismay lifted in some degree from my wits. I filled my glass and looked at it against the fire-glow, and dreamed that 'twas an emblem of the after course of my life. Who knew what fine things I might come to yet, though now I was solitary in a strange land?

The landlord came in and took away the remnants himself. He looked at me fixedly more than once, and in his glance I read madness, greed, and hatred. I feared his look, and was glad to see him leave, for he made me feel angry and a little awed. However, thought I, 'tis not the first time I have met a churlish host, and I filled my glass again.

The fire bickered cheerily, lighting up the room and comforting my cold skin. I drew my chair close and stretched out my legs to the blaze, till in a little, betwixt heat and weariness, I was pleasantly drowsy. I fell to thinking of the events of the day and the weary road I had travelled; then to an earlier time, when I first came to Scotland, and my hopes were still unbroken. After all this I began to mind me of the pleasant days in France; for, though I had often fared ill enough there, all was forgotten but the good fortune; and I had soon built out of my brain a France which was liker Paradise than anywhere on earth. Every now and then a log would crackle or fall, and so wake me with a start, for the fire was of that sort which is common in hilly places—a great bank of peat with wood laid athwart. Blue, pungent smoke came out in rings and clouds, which smelt gratefully in my nostrils after the black out-of-doors.

By-and-bye, what with thinking of the past, what with my present comfort, and what with an ever-hopeful imagination, my prospects came to look less dismal. 'Twas true that I was here in a most unfriendly land with little money and no skill of the country. But Scotland was but a little place after all. I must come to Leith in time, where I could surely meet a French skipper who would take me over, money or no. You will ask, whoever may chance to read this narrative, why, in Heaven's name, I did not turn and go back to Ayr, the port from which I had come? The reason is not far to seek. The whole land behind me stank in my nostrils, for there dwelt Quentin Kennedy, and there lay the scene of my discomfiture and my sufferings. Faugh! the smell of that wretched moor-road is with me yet. So, with thinking one way and another, I came to a decision to go forward in any case, and trust to God and my own good fortune. After this I must have ceased to have any thoughts, and dropped off snugly to sleep.

I wakened, at what time I know not, shivering, with a black fire before my knees. The room was black with darkness, save where through a chink in the window-shutter there came a gleam of pale moonlight. I sprang up in haste, and called for a servant to show me to my sleeping-room, but the next second I could have wished the word back, for I feared that no servant would be awake and at hand. To my mind there seemed something passing strange in thus leaving a guest to slumber by the fire.

To my amazement, the landlord himself came to my call, bearing a light in his hand. I was reasonably surprised, for though I knew not the hour of the night, I judged from the state of the fire that it must have been far advanced.

"I had fallen asleep," I said in apology, "and now would finish what I have begun. Show me my bed."

"It'll be a dark nicht and a coorse, out-bye," said the man, as he led the way solemnly from the room, up a rickety stair, down a mirk passage to a chamber which, from the turnings of the house, I guessed to be facing the east. 'Twas a comfortless place, and ere I could add a word I found the man leaving the room with the light. "You'll find your way to bed in the dark," quoth he, and I was left in blackness.

I sat down on the edge of the bed, half-stupid with sleep, my teeth chattering with the cold, listening to the gusts of wind battering against the little window. Faith! I thought, this is the worst entertainment I ever had, and I have made trial of many. Yet I need not complain, for I have had a good fire and a royal supper, and my present discomfort is due in great part to my own ill habit of drowsiness. I rose to undress, for my bones were sore after the long day's riding, when, by some chance, I moved forward to the window and opened it to look on the night.

'Twas wintry weather outside, though but the month of August. The face of the hills fronting me were swathed in white mist, which hung low even to the banks of the stream. There was a great muttering in the air of swollen

water, for the rain had ceased, and the red waves were left
to roll down the channel to the lowlands and make havoc of
meadow and steading. The sky was cumbered with clouds,
and no clear light of the moon came through; but since
'twas nigh the time of the full moon the night was not ut-
terly dark.

I lingered for maybe five minutes in this posture, and
then I heard that which made me draw in my head and listen the more intently. A thud of horses' hoofs on the wet
ground came to my ear. A second, and it was plainer, the
noise of some half-dozen riders clearly approaching the
inn. 'Twas a lonesome place, and I judged it strange that
company should come so late.

I flung myself on the bed in my clothes, and could almost have fallen asleep as I was, so weary was my body. But
there was that in my mind which forbade slumber, a vague
uneasiness as of some ill approaching, which it behoved
me to combat. Again and again I tried to drive it from me
as mere cowardice, but again it returned to vex me. There
was nothing for it but that I should lie on my back and bide
what might come.

Then again I heard a sound, this time from a room beneath. 'Twas as if men were talking softly, and moving to
and fro. My curiosity was completely aroused, and I thought
it no shame to my soldierly honour to slip from my room
and gather what was the purport of their talk. At such a
time, and in such a place, it boded no good for me, and the
evil face of the landlord was ever in my memory. The staircase creaked a little as it felt my weight, but it had been built
for heavier men, and I passed it in safety. Clearly the visitors
were in the room where I had supped.

"Will we ha'e muckle wark wi' him, think ye," I heard
one man ask.

"Na, na," said another, whom I knew for mine host.

"he's a foreigner, a man frae a fremt land, and a' folk ken they're little use. Forbye, I had stock o' him mysel', and I think I could mak his bit ribs crack thegither. He'll no' be an ill customer to deal wi'.'"

"But will he no' be a guid hand at the swird? There's no yin o' us here muckle at that."

"Toots," said another, "we'll e'en get him intil a corner, where he'll no git leave to stir an airm."

I had no stomach for more. With a dull sense of fear I crept back to my room, scarce heeding in my anger whether I made noise or not. Good God! thought I, I have travelled by land and sea to die in a moorland alehouse by the hand of common robbers! My heart grew hot at the thought of the landlord, for I made no doubt that it was my jewels that had first set his teeth. I loosened my sword in its scabbard; and now I come to think of it, 'twas a great wonder that it had not been taken from me while I slept. I could only guess that the man had been afraid to approach me before the arrival of his confederates. I gripped my sword-hilt; ah! how often had I felt its touch under kindlier circumstances—when I slew the boar in the woods at Belnot, when I made the Sieur de Biran crave pardon before my feet, when I—but peace with such memories! At all events, if Jean de Rohaine must die among ruffians, unknown and forgotten, he would finish his days like a gentleman of courage. I prayed to God that I might only have the life of the leader.

But this world is sweet to all men, and as I awaited death in that dark room, it seemed especially fair to live. I was but in the prime of my age, on the near side of forty, hale in body, a master of the arts and graces. Were it not passing hard that I should perish in this wise? I looked every way for a means of escape. There was but one—the little window which looked upon the ground east of the inn. 'Twas just conceivable that a man might leap it and make his way to the hills, and so baffle his pursuers. Two thoughts deterred me; first, that I had no horse and could not continue my journey; second, that in all likelihood there would be a watch set below. My heart sank within me, and I ceased to think.

For, just at that moment, I heard a noise below as of men leaving the room. I shut my lips and waited. Here, I concluded, is death coming to meet me. But the next moment the noise had stopped, and 'twas evident that the conclave was not yet closed. 'Tis a strange thing the mind of man, for I, who had looked with despair at my chances a minute agone, now, at the passing of this immediate danger, plucked up heart, clapped my hat on my head, and opened the window.

The night air blew chill, but all seemed silent below. So very carefully I hung over the ledge, gripped the sill with my hands, swung my legs into the air, and dropped. I lighted on a tussock of grass and rolled over on my side, only to recover myself in an instant and rise to my feet, and, behold, at my side, a tall man keeping sentinel on horseback.

At this the last flicker of hope died in my bosom. The man never moved or spake, but only stared fixedly at me. Yet there was that in his face and bearing which led me to act as I did.

"If you are a man of honour," I burst out, "though you are engaged in an accursed trade, dismount and meet me in combat. Your spawn will not be out for a little time, and the night is none so dark. If I must die, I would die at least in the open air, with my foe before me."

My words must have found some answering chord in the man's breast, for he presently spoke, and asked me my name and errand in the countryside. I told him in a dozen words, and at my tale he shrugged his shoulders.

"I am in a great mind," says he, "to let you go. I am

all but sick of this butcher work, and would fling it to the winds at a word. 'Tis well enough for the others who are mongrel bred, but it ill becomes a man of birth like me, who am own cousin to the Maxwells o' Drurie."

He fell for a very little time into a sort of musing, tugging at his beard like a man in perplexity. Then he spake out suddenly—

"See you yon tuft of willows by the water? There's a space behind it where a horse and man might stand well concealed. There is your horse," and he pointed to a group of horses standing tethered by the roadside; "lead him to the place I speak of, and trust to God for the rest. I will raise a scare that you're off the other airt, and, mind, that whenever you see the tails o' us, you mount and ride for life in the way I tell you. You should win to Drumlanrig by morning, where there are quieter folk. Now, mind my bidding, and dae't before my good will changes."

"May God do so to you in your extremity! If ever I meet you on earth I will repay you for your mercy. But a word with you. Who is that man?" and I pointed to the house.

The fellow laughed dryly. "It's easy seen you're no acquaint here or you would ha' heard o' Long Jock o' the Hirsel. There's mony a man would face the devil wi' a regiment o' dragoons at his back, that would flee at a glint from Jock's een. You're weel quit o' him. But be aff afore the folk are stirring."

I needed no second bidding, but led Saladin with all speed to the willows, where I made him stand knee-deep in the water within cover of the trees, while I crouched by his side. 'Twas none too soon, for I was scarce in hiding when I heard a great racket in the house, and the sound of men swearing and mounting horse. There was a loud clattering of hoofs; which shortly died away, and left the world quiet, save for the broil of the stream and the loud screaming of moor-birds.

III.

I FARE BADLY ABROAD.

ALL this has taken a long time to set down, but there was little time in the acting. Scarce half-an-hour had passed from my waking by the black fire till I found myself up to the waist in the stream. I made no further delay, but, as soon as the air was quiet, led Saladin out as stilly as I could on the far side of the willows, clambered on his back (for I was too sore in body to mount in any other fashion), and was riding for dear life along the moor-road in the contrary direction to that from which I had come on the night before. The horse had plainly been well fed, since, doubtless, the ruffians had marked him for their own plunder. He covered the ground in gallant fashion, driving up jets and splashes of rain-water from the pools in the way. Mile after mile was passed with no sound of pursuers; one hill gave place to another; the stream grew wider and more orderly; but still I kept up the breakneck pace, fearing to slacken rein. Fifteen miles were covered, as I judged, before I saw the first light of dawn in the sky, a red streak in a gray desert; and brought my horse down to a trot, thanking God that at last I was beyond danger.

I was sore in body, with clammy garments sticking to my skin, aching in back and neck, unslept, well-nigh as miserable as a man could be. But great as was my bodily discomfort, 'twas not one tittle to compare with the sickness of my heart. I had been driven to escape from a hostel by a window like a common thief; compelled to ride—nay,

there was no use in disguising it—to flee, before a pack of
ill-bred villains; I, a gentleman of France, who had ruffled
it with the best of them in my fit of prosperity. Again and
again I questioned with myself whether I had not done better to die in that place, fighting as long as the breath was in
my body. Of this I am sure, at any rate, that it would have
been the way more soothing to my pride. I argued the matter with myself, according to the most approved logic, but
could come no nearer to the solution. For while I thought
the picture of myself dying with my back to the wall the
more heroical and gentleman-like, it yet went sore against
me to think of myself, with all my skill of the sword and the
polite arts, perishing in a desert place at the hand of common cut-throats. 'Twas no fear of death, I give my word
of honour; that was a weakness never found in our race.
Courage is a virtue I take no credit for; 'tis but a matter
of upbringing. But a man loves to make some noise in the
earth ere he leaves it, or at least to pass with blowings of the
trumpet and some manner of show. To this day I cannot
think of any way by which I could have mended my conduct. I can but set it down as a mischance of Providence,
which meets all men in their career, but of which no man
of spirit cares to think.

The sun rose clear, but had scarce shone for an hour,
when, as is the way in this land, a fresh deluge of rain came
on, and the dawn which had begun in crimson ended in a
dull level of gray. I had never been used with much foul
weather of this sort, so I bore it ill. 'Twas about nine of
the morning when I rode into the village of Drumlanrig,
a jumble of houses in the lee of a great wood, which runs
up to meet the descending moorlands. Some ragged brats,
heedless of the weather, played in the street, if one may
call it by so fine a name; but for the most part the houses
seemed quite deserted. A woman looked incuriously at me;

a man who was carrying sacks scarce raised his head to
view me; the whole place was like a dwelling of the dead. I
have since learned the reason, which was no other than the
accursed butchery on which I had quarrelled with Quentin
Kennedy, and so fallen upon misfortune. The young and
manly were all gone; some to the hills for hiding, some to
the town prisons, some across the seas to work in the plan-
tations, and some on that long journey from which no man
returns. My heart boils within me to this day to think of
it—but there! it is long since past, and I have little need to
be groaning over it now.

There was no inn in the place, but I bought bread from
the folk of a little farm-steading at one end of the village
street. They would scarce give it me at first, and 'twas not
till they beheld my woebegone plight that their hearts re-
lented. Doubtless they took me for one of the soldiers who
had harried them and theirs, little guessing that 'twas all for
their sake that I was in such evil case. I did not tarry to ask
the road, for Leith was too far distant for the people in that
place to know it. Of this much I was sure, that it lay to the
north-east, so I took my way in that direction, shaping my
course by the sun. There was a little patch of green fields,
a clump of trees, and a quiet stream beside the village; but
I had scarce ridden half a mile beyond it when once more
the moor swallowed me up in its desert of moss and wet
heather.

I was now doubly dispirited. My short exhilaration of
escape had gone, and all the pangs of wounded pride and
despair seized upon me, mingled with a sort of horror at
the place I had come through. Whenever I saw a turn of hill
which brought the *Angel's Ladder* to my mind, I shivered in
spite of myself, and could have found it in my heart to turn
and flee. In addition, I would have you remember, I was
soaked to the very skin, my eyes weary with lack of sleep,

and my legs cramped with much riding. The place in the main was moorland, with steep, desolate hills on my left. On the right to the south I had glimpses of a fairer country, woods and distant fields, seen for an instant through the driving mist. In a trice France was back in my mind, for I could not see an acre of green land without coming nigh to tears. Yet, and perhaps 'twas fortunate for me, such glimpses were all too rare. For the most part, the way was a long succession of sloughs and mires, with here a piece of dry, heathy ground, and there an impetuous water coming down from the highlands. Saladin soon fell tired, and, indeed, small wonder, since he had come many miles, and his fare had been of the scantiest. He would put his foot in a bog-hole and stumble so sharply that I would all but lose my seat. Then, poor beast, he would take shame to himself, and pick his way as well as his weary legs would suffer him. 'Twas an evil plight for man and steed, and I knew not which to pity the more.

At noon, I came to the skirts of a long hill, whose top was hidden with fog, but which I judged to be high and lonesome. I met a man—the first I had seen since Drumlanrig—and asked him my whereabouts. I learned that the hill was called Queen's Berry, and that in some dozen miles I would strike the high road to Edinburgh. I could get not another word out of him, but must needs content myself with this crumb of knowledge. The road in front was no road, nothing but a heathery moor, with walls of broken stones seaming it like the lines of sewing in an old coat. Grey broken hills came up for a minute, as a stray wind blew the mist aside, only to disappear the next instant in a ruin of cloud.

From this place I mark the beginning of the most wretched journey in my memory. Till now I had had some measure of bodily strength to support me. Now it failed,

and a cold shivering fit seized on my vitals, and more than
once I was like to have fallen from my horse. A great stupid-
ity came over my brain; I could call up no remembrance to
cheer me, but must plod on in a horror of darkness. The
cause was not far distant—cold, wet, and despair. I tried to
swallow some of the rain-soaked bread in my pouch, but
my mouth was as dry as a skin. I dismounted to drink at a
stream, but the water could hardly trickle down my throat
so much did it ache. 'Twas as if I were on the eve of an
ague, and in such a place it were like to be the end of me.

Had there been a house, I should have craved shelter. But
one effect of my sickness was, that I soon strayed wofully
from my path, such as it was, and found myself in an evil
case with bogs and steep hillsides. I had much to do in keeping Saladin from danger; and had I not felt the obligation
to behave like a man, I should have flung the reins on his
neck and let him bear himself and his master to destruc-
tion. Again and again I drove the wish from my mind—"As
well die in a bog-hole or break your neck over a crag as
dwine away with ague in the cold heather, as you are like
to do," said the tempter. But I steeled my heart, and made
a great resolve to keep one thing, though I should lose all
else—some shreds of my manhood.

Towards evening I grew so ill that I was fain, when we
came to a level place, to lay my head on Saladin's neck and
let him stumble forward. My head swam, and my back
ached so terribly, that I guessed feverishly that someone
had stabbed me unawares. The weather cleared just about
even, and the light of day flickered out in a watery sunset.
'Twas like the close of my life, I thought, a grey ill day and
a poor ending. The notion depressed me miserably. I felt a
kinship with that feeble evening light, a kinship begotten
of equality in weakness. However, all would soon end; my
day must presently have its evening; and then, if all tales

were true, and my prayers had any efficacy, I should be in a better place.

But when once the night in its blackness had set in, I longed for the light again, however dismal it might be. A ghoulish song, one which I had heard long before, was ever coming to my memory—

> "La pluye nous a debuez et lavez,
>   Et le soleil dessechez et noirciz;
>   Pies, corbeaux————"

With a sort of horror I tried to drive it from my mind. A dreadful heaviness oppressed me. Fears, which I am ashamed to set down, thronged my brain. The way had grown easier, or I make no doubt my horse had fallen. 'Twas a track we were on, I could tell by the greater freedom with which Saladin stepped. God send, I prayed, that we be near to folk, and that they be kindly; this prayer I said many times to the accompaniment of the whistling of the doleful wind. Every gust pained me. I was the sport of the weather, a broken puppet tossed about by circumstance.

Now an answer was sent to me, and that a speedy one. I came of a sudden to a clump of shrubbery beside a wall. Then at a turn of the way a light shone through, as from a broad window among trees. A few steps more and I stumbled on a gate and turned Saladin's head up a pathway. The rain dripped heavily from the bushes, a branch slashed me in the face, and my weariness grew tenfold with every second. I dropped like a log before the door, scarce looking to see whether the house was great or little; and, ere I could knock or make any call, swooned away dead on the threshold.

IV.

OF MY COMING TO LINDEAN.

WHEN I came to myself I was lying in a pleasant room with a great flood of sunlight drifting through the window. My brain was so confused that it was many minutes ere I could guess in which part of the earth I was laid. My first thought was that I was back in France, and I rejoiced with a great gladness; but, as my wits cleared, the past came back by degrees, till I had it plain before me, from my setting-out to my fainting at the door. Clearly I was in the house where I had arrived on the even of yesterday.

I stirred, and found my weakness gone, and my health, save for some giddiness in the head, quite recovered. This was ever the way of our family, who may be in the last desperation one day and all alive and active the next. Our frames are like the old grape tendrils, slim but tough as whipcord.

At my first movement some one arose from another part of the room and came forward. I looked with curiosity, and found that it was a girl, who brought me some strengthening food-stuff in a bowl. The sunlight smote her full in the face and set her hair all aglow, as if she were the Madonna. I could not see her well, but, as she bent over me, she seemed tall and lithe and pretty to look upon.

"How feel you?" she asked in a strange, soft accent, speaking the pure English, but with a curious turn in her voice. "I trust you are better of your ailment."

"Yes, that I am," I said briskly, for I was ashamed to

be lying there in good health, "and I would thank you, Mademoiselle, for your courtesy to a stranger."

"Nay, nay," she cried, "'twas but common humanity. You were sore spent last night, both man and horse. Had you travelled far? But no," she added hastily, seeing me about to plunge into a narrative; "your tale will keep. I cannot have you making yourself ill again. You had better bide still a little longer." And with a deft hand she arranged the pillows and was gone.

For some time I lay in a pleasing inaction. 'Twas plain I had fallen among gentlefolk, and I blessed the good fortune which had led me to the place. Here I might find one to hear my tale and help me in my ill-luck. At anyrate for the present I was in a good place, and when one has been living in a nightmare, the present has the major part in his thoughts. With this I fell asleep again, for I was still somewhat wearied in body.

When I awoke 'twas late afternoon. The evil weather seemed to have gone, for the sun was bright and the sky clear with the mellowness of approaching even. The girl came again and asked me how I fared. "For," said she, "perhaps you wish to rise if you are stronger. Your clothes were sadly wet and torn when we got you to bed last night, so my father has bade me ask you to accept of another suit till your own may be in better order. See, I have laid them out for you, if you will put them on." And again, ere I could thank her, she was gone.

I was surprised and somewhat affected by this crowning kindness, and at the sight of so much care for a stranger whose very name was unknown. I longed to meet at once with the men of the house, so I sprung up and drew the clothes towards me. They were of rough gray cloth, very strong and warm, and fitting a man a little above the ordinary height, of such stature as mine is. It did not take me many minutes to dress, and when once more I found myself arrayed in wholesome garments I felt my spirit returning, and with it came hope and a kindlier outlook on the world.

No one appeared, so I opened my chamber door and found myself at the head of a staircase, which turned steeply down almost from the threshold. A great window illumined it, and many black-framed pictures hung on the walls adown it. At the foot there was a hall, broad and low in the roof, whence some two or three doors opened. Sounds of men in conversation came from one, so I judged it wise to turn there. With much curiosity I lifted the latch and entered unbidden.

'Twas a little room, well-furnished and stocked to the very ceiling with books. A fire burned on the hearth, by which sat two men talking. They rose to their feet as I entered, and I marked them well. One was an elderly man of maybe sixty years, with a bend in his back as if from study. His face was narrow and kindly; blue eyes, like a Northman, a thin, twitching lip, and hair well turned to silver. His companion was scarce less notable—a big, comely man, dressed half in the fashion of a soldier, yet with the air of one little versed in cities. I love to be guessing a man's station from his looks, and ere I had glanced him over, I had set him down in my mind as a country *laird*, as these folk call it. Both greeted me courteously, and then, as I advanced, were silent, as if waiting for me to give some account of myself.

"I have come to thank you for your kindness," said I awkwardly, "and to let you know something of myself, for 'tis ill to be harbouring folk without names or dwelling."

"Tush," said the younger, "'twere a barbarity to leave anyone without so travel-worn as you. The Levite in the Scriptures did no worse. But how feel you now? I trust your fatigue is gone."

"I thank you a thousand times for your kindness. Would I knew how to repay it!"

"Nay, young man," said the elder, "give thanks not to us, but to the Lord who led you to this place. The moors are hard bedding, and right glad I am that you fell in with us here. 'Tis seldom we have a stranger with us, since my brother at Drumlanrig died in the spring o' last year. But I trust you are better, and that Anne has looked after you well. A maid is a blessing to sick folk, if a weariness to the hale."

"You speak truly," I said, "a maid is a blessing to the sick. 'Tis sweet to be well tended when you have fared hardly for days. Your kindness has set me at peace with the world again. Yesterday all was black before me, and now, I bethink me, I see a little ray of light."

"'Twas a good work," said the old man, "to give you hope and set you right with yourself, if so chance we have done it. What saith the wise man, 'He that hath no rule over his own spirit is like a city that is broken down and without walls?' But whence have you come? We would hear your story."

So I told them the whole tale of my wanderings, from my coming to Kennedy to my fainting fit at their own threshold. At the story of my quarrel they listened eagerly, and I could mark their eyes flashing, and as I spake of my sufferings in the desert I could see sympathy in their faces. When I concluded, neither spake for a little, till the elder man broke silence with—

"May God bless and protect you in all your goings! Well I see that you are of the upright in heart. It makes me blithe to have you in my house."

The younger said nothing but rose and came to me.

"M. de Rohaine," he said, speaking my name badly, "give me your hand. I honour you for a gentleman and a man of feeling."

"And I am glad to give it you," said I, and we clasped
hands and looked into each other's eyes. Then we stepped
back well satisfied. For myself I love to meet a man, and in
the great-limbed young fellow before me I found one to my
liking.

"And now I must tell you of ourselves," said the old man,
"for 'tis fitting that a guest should know his entertainers.
This is the manse of Lindean, and I am the unworthy man,
Ephraim Lambert, whom God hath appointed to watch
over His flock in this place. Sore, sore are we troubled by
evil men, such as you have known; and my folk, from dwelling in decent cots, have to hide in peat-hags and the caves
of the hills. The Lord's hand is heavy upon this country; 'tis
a time of trial, a passing through the furnace. God grant
we be not found faithless! This home is still left to us, and
thankful we should be for it; and I demand that you dwell
with us till you have settled on your course. This man," he
went on, laying his hand on the shoulder of the younger, "is
Master Henry Semple of Clachlands, a fine inheritance, all
ridden and rieved by these devils on earth, Captain Keith's
dragoons. Henry is of our belief, and a man of such mettle
that the Privy Council was fain to send down a quartering
of soldiers to bide in his house and devour his substance.
'Twas a thing no decent man could thole, so off he comes
here to keep us company till the wind blows by. If you look
out of the window over by the side of yon rig of hill, ye'll
get a glimmer of Clachlands chimneys, reeking with the
smoke of their evil preparations. Ay, ay, lads, burn you your
peats and fill up the fire with logs till the vent's choked,
but you'll burn brawly yourselves some fine day, when your
master gives you your wages." He looked out as he spoke,
and into his kindly eyes came a gleam of such anger and decision as quite transfigured his face and made it seem more
like that of a troop captain than a peaceful minister.

And now Master Semple spoke up: "God send, sir, they suffer for no worse a crime than burning my peats and firewood. I should count myself a sorry fellow if I made any complaint about a little visitation, when the hand of the Lord is smiting so sorely among my fellows. I could take shame to myself every time I eat good food or sleep in a decent bed, to think of better men creeping aneath the lang heather like etherts or shivering on the cauld hill-side. There'll be no such doings in your land, M. de Rohaine? I've heard tell of folk there like us, dwelling in the hills to escape the abominations of Rome. But, perhaps," and he hesitated, "you are not of them?"

"No," said I, "I am of your enemies by upbringing; but I dearly love a brave man, wherever I meet him. 'Tis poor religion, say I, which would lead one to see no virtue in those of another belief. There is one God above all."

"Ay, you speak truly," said the old man; "He has made of one blood all the nations of the earth. But I yearn to see you of a better way of thinking. Mayhap I may yet show you your errors?"

"I thank you, but I hold by 'every man to his upbringing.' Each man to the creed of his birth. 'Tis a poor thing to be changing on any pretext. For, look you, God, who appointed a man his place of birth, set him his religion with it, and I hold if he but stick to it he is not far in error." I spoke warmly, but in truth I had thought all too little about such things. One who has to fight his way among men and live hardly, has, of necessity, little time for his devotions, and if he but live cleanly, his part is well done. *Mon Dieu!* Who will gainsay me?

"I fear your logic is faulty," said Master Semple, "but it is mighty inhospitable to be arguing with a guest. See, here Anne comes with the lamp, and supper will soon be ready."

The girl came in as he spake, bearing a great lamp, which she placed on a high shelf, and set about laying the table for supper. I had noticed her little at first sight, for I was never given to staring at maids; but now, as she moved about, I found myself ever watching her. The ruddy firelight striving with the serene glow of the lamp met and flickered about her face and hair. She was somewhat brown in skin, like a country maiden; but there was no semblance of rusticity in her fair features and deep brown eyes. Her hair hung over her neck as brown as the soft fur of a squirrel, and the fire filled it with fantastic shadows. She was singularly grace-ful in figure, moving through the room and bending over the table with a grace which 'twas pretty to contemplate. 'Twas strange to note that when her face was averted one might have guessed her to be some village girl or burgher's daughter; but as soon as she had turned her imperial eyes on you she looked like a queen in a play. Her face was a cu-rious one, serious and dignified beyond her years and sex, yet with odd sparkles of gaiety dancing in her eyes and the corners of her rosy mouth.

Master Semple had set about helping her, and a pretty sight it was to see her reproving and circumventing his clumsiness. 'Twas not hard to see the relation between the two. The love-light shone in his eye whenever he looked to-ward her; and she, for her part, seemed to thrill at his chance touch. One strange thing I noted, that, whereas in France two young folks could not have gone about the business of setting a supper-table without much laughter and frolic, all was done here as if 'twere some solemn ceremonial.

To one who was still sick with the thought of the black uplands he had traversed, of the cold, driving rain and the deadly bogs, the fare in the manse was like the apple to Eve in the garden. 'Twas fine to be eating crisp oaten cakes and butter fresh from the churn, to be drinking sweet warm milk—for we lived on the plainest; and, above all, to watch kindly faces around you in place of marauders and low ruffians. The minister said a lengthy grace before and after the meal; and when the table was cleared the servants were called in to evening prayer. Again the sight pleased me—the two maids with their brown country faces seated decently by the door; Anne half in shadow sitting demurely with Master Semple not far off, and at the table-head the white hairs of the old man bowed over the Bible. He read I know not what, for I am not so familiar with the Scriptures as I should be, and, moreover, Anne's grave face was a more entrancing study. Then we knelt, and he prayed to God to watch over us in all our ways and bring us at last to His prepared kingdom. Truly, when I arose from my knees, I felt more tempted to be devout than I have any remembrance of before.

Then we sat and talked of this and that, and I must tell over all my misfortunes again for mademoiselle's entertainment. She listened with open wonder, and thanked me with her marvellous eyes. Then to bed with a vile-smelling lamp, in a wide, low-ceilinged sleeping-room, where the sheets were odorous of bog-myrtle and fresh as snow. Sleep is a goddess easy of conquest when wooed in such a fashion.

V.

I PLEDGE MY WORD.

OF my life at Lindean for the next three days I have
no clear remembrance. The weather was dry and lan-
guid, as often follows a spell of rain, and the long hills which
huddled around the house looked near and imminent. The
place was so still that if one shouted it seemed almost a
profanation. 'Twas so Sabbath-like that I almost came to
dislike it. Indeed, I doubt I should have found it irksome,
had there not been a brawling stream in the glen which
kept up a continuous dashing and chattering. It seemed the
one link between me and that far-away world in which not
long agone I had been a dweller.

The life, too, was as regular as in the king's court. Sharp
at six I was awakened, and ere seven we were assembled for
breakfast. Then to prayers, and then to the occupations of the
day. The minister would be at his books or down among his
people on some errand of mercy. The church had been long
closed, for the Privy Council, seeing that Master Lambert
was opposed to them, had commanded him to be silent; and
yet, mark you, so well was he loved in the place, that they
durst set no successor in his stead. They tried it once and a
second time, but the unhappy man was so taken with fear
of the people that he shook the dust of Lindean off his feet,
and departed in search of a more hospitable dwelling. But
the minister's mouth was shut, save when covertly, and with
the greatest peril to himself, he would preach at a meeting
of the hill-folk in the recesses of the surrounding uplands.

The library I found no bad one—I who in my day have
been considered to have something of a taste in books. To
be sure, there was much wearisome stuff, the work of old di-
vines, and huge commentaries on the Scriptures, written in
Latin and plentifully interspersed with Greek and Hebrew.
But there was good store of the Classics, both prose and po-
etry,—*Horace*, who has ever been my favourite, and *Homer*,
who, to my thinking, is the finest of the ancients. Here,
too, I found a *Plato*, and I swear I read more of him in the
manse than I have done since I went through him with M.
Clerselier, when we were students together in Paris.

The acquaintance which I had formed with Master
Semple speedily ripened into a fast friendship. I found it in
my heart to like this great serious man—a bumpkin if you
will, but a man of courage and kindliness. We were wont
to take long walks, always in some lonely part of the country, and we grew more intimate in our conversation than I
should ever have dreamed of. He would call me John, and
this much I suffered him, to save my name from the barbarity of his pronunciation; while in turn I fell to calling
him Henry, as if we had been born and bred together. I
found that he loved to hear of my own land and my past
life, which, now that I think of it, must have had no little
interest to one dwelling in such solitudes. From him I heard
of his father, of his brief term at the College of Edinburgh,
which he left when the strife in the country grew high,
and of his sorrow and anger at the sufferings of those who
withstood the mandate of the King. Though I am of the
true faith, I think it no shame that my sympathy was all
with these rebels, for had I not seen something of their mis-
ery myself? But, above all, he would speak of *la belle Anne* as
one gentleman will tell another of his love, when he found
that I was a willing listener. I could scarce have imagined
such warmth of passion to exist in the man as he showed at

the very mention of her name. "Oh!" he would cry out, "I would die for her; I would gang to the world's end to pleasure her. I whiles think that I break the first commandment every day of my life, for I canna keep her a moment out of my thoughts, and I fear she's more to me than any earthly thing should be. I think of her at nicht. I see her name in every page of the Book. I thought I was bad when I was over at Clachlands, and had to ride five miles to see her; but now I'm tenfold worse when I'm biding aside her. God grant it be not counted to me for sin!"

"Amen to that," said I. 'Tis a fine thing to see the love of a maid; but I hold 'tis a finer to witness the passion of a strong man.

Yet, withal, there was something sinister about the house and its folk which to me was the fly in the ointment. They were kindness and charity incarnate, but they were cold and gloomy to boot, lacking any grace or sprightliness in their lives. I find it hard to write this, for their goodness to me was beyond recompense; yet I must set it down, since in some measure it has to do with my story. The old man would look at me at times and sigh, nor did I think it otherwise than fitting, till I found from his words that the sighs were on account of my own spiritual darkness. I have no quarrel with any man for wishing to convert me, but to sigh at one's approach seems a doleful way of setting about it. Then he would break out from his wonted quietness at times to rail at his foes, calling down the wrath of Heaven to blight them. Such a fit was always followed by a painful exhaustion, which left him as weak as a child, and shivering like a leaf. I bitterly cursed the state of a country which could ruin the peace of mind of a man so sweet-tempered by nature, and make him the sport of needless rage. 'Twas pitiful to see him creep off to his devotions after any such outbreak, penitent and ashamed. Even to his daughter he

was often cruelly sharp, and would call her to account for
the merest trifle.

As for Master Henry, what shall I say of him? I grew to
love him like my own brother, yet I no more understood him
than the Sultan of Turkey. He had strange fits of gloom, begotten, I must suppose, of the harsh country and his many
anxieties, in which he was more surly than a bear, speaking
little, and that mainly from the Scriptures. I have one case in
my memory, when, had I not been in a sense his guest, I had
scarce refrained from quarrelling. 'Twas in the afternoon of
the second day, when we returned weary from one of our
long wanderings. Anne tripped forth into the autumn sunlight singing a catch, a simple glee of the village folk.

"Peace, Anne," says Master Henry savagely; "it little becomes you to be singing in these days, unless it be a godly
psalm. Keep your songs for better times."

"What ails you?" I ventured to say. "You praised her this
very morning for singing the self-same verses."

"And peace, you," he says roughly, as he entered the
house; "if the lass hearkened to your accursed creed, I
should have stronger words for her."

My breath was fairly taken from me at this incredible
rudeness. I had my hand on my sword, and had I been in
my own land we should soon have settled it. As it was, I
shut my lips firmly and choked down my choler.

Yet I cannot leave with this ill word of the man. That very
night he talked with me so pleasingly, and with so friendly a
purport, that I conceived he must have been scarce himself
when he so insulted me. Indeed, I discerned two natures
in the man—one, hard, saturnine, fanatically religious; the
other, genial and kindly, like that of any other gentleman
of family. The former I attributed to the accident of his fortune; the second I held to be the truer, and in my thoughts
of him still think of it as the only one.

But I must pass to the events which befell on the even of the third day, and wrought so momentous a change in the life at Lindean. 'Twas just at the lighting of the lamp, when Anne and the minister and myself sat talking in the little sitting-room, that Master Henry entered with a look of great concern on his face, and beckoned the elder man out.

"Andrew Gibb is here," said he.

"And what may Andrew Gibb be wanting?" asked the old man, glancing up sharply.

"He brings nae guid news, I fear, but he'll tell them to none but you; so hasten out, sir, to the back, for he's come far, and he's ill at the waiting."

The twain were gone for some time, and in their absence I could hear high voices in the back end of the house, conversing as on some matter of deep import. Anne fetched the lamp from the kitchen and trimmed it with elaborate care, lighting it and setting it in its place. Then, at last, the minister returned alone.

I was shocked at the sight of him as he re-entered the room. His face was ashen pale and tightly drawn about the lips. He crept to a chair and leaned his head on the table, speaking no word. Then he burst out of a sudden into a storm of pleading.

"O Lord God," he cried, "Thou hast aye been good to us, Thou hast kept us weel, and bielded us frae the wolves who have sought to devour us. Oh, dinna leave us now. It's no' for mysel' or Henry that I care. We're men, and can warstle through ills; but oh, what am I to dae wi' the bit helpless lassie? It's awfu' to have to gang oot among hills and bogs to bide, but it's ten times waur when ye dinna ken what's gaun to come to your bairn. Hear me, O Lord, and grant me my request. I've no' been a' that I micht have been, but oh, if I ha'e tried to serve Thee at a', dinna let this danger overwhelm us!"

He had scarcely finished, and was still sitting with bowed head, when Master Henry also entered the room. His eyes were filled with an austere frenzy, such as I had learned to look for.

"Ay, sir," said he, "'tis a time for us a' to be on our knees. But ha'e courage, and dinna let us spoil the guid cause by our weak mortal complaining. Is't no' better to be hunkering in a moss-hole and communing with the Lord than waxing fat like Jeshurun in carnal corruption? Call on God's name, but no' wi' sighing, but wi' exaltation, for He hath bidden us to a mighty heritage."

"Ye speak brave and true, Henry, and I'm wi' your every word. But tell me what's to become o' my bairn? What will Anne dae? I once thought there was something atween you——" He stopped abruptly, and searched the face of the young man.

At his words Master Semple had started as under a lash. "O my God," he cried, "I had forgotten. Anne, Anne, my dearie, we canna leave ye, and you to be my wife. This is a sore trial of faith, sir, and I misdoubt I canna stand it. To leave ye to the tender mercies o' a' the hell-hounds o' dragoons—oh! I canna dae't." He clapped his hand to his forehead and walked about the room like a man distraught.

And now I put in my word. "What ails you, Henry? Tell me, for I am sore grieved to see you in such perplexity."

"Ails me?" he repeated. "Aye, I will tell ye what ails me"; and he drew his chair before me. "Andrew Gibb's come ower frae the Ruthen wi' shure news that a warrant's oot against us baith, for being at the preaching on Callowa' Muir. 'Twas an enemy did it, and now the soldiers are coming at ony moment to lay hands on us and take us off to Embro'. Then there'll be but a short lease of life for us; and unless we take to the hills this very nicht, we may be ower late in the morning. I'm wae to tak' sae auld a man as

Master Lambert to wet mosses, but there's nothing else to be dune. But what's to become o' Anne? Whae's to see to her, when the dragoons come riding and cursing about the toon? Oh, it's a terrible time, John. Pray to God, if ye never prayed before, to let it pass."

Mademoiselle had meantime spoken never a word, but had risen and gone to her father's chair and put her arms around his neck. Her presence seemed to cheer the old man, for he ceased mourning and looked up, while she sat, still as a statue, with her grave, lovely face against his. But Master Semple's grief was pitiful to witness. He rocked himself to and fro in his chair, with his arms folded and a set, white face. Every now and then he would break into a cry like a stricken animal. The elder man was the first to counsel patience.

"Stop, Henry," says he; "it's ill befitting Christian folk to set sic an example. We've a' got our troubles, and if ours are heavier than some, it's no' for us to complain. Think o' the many years o' grace we've had. There's nae doubt the Lord will look after the bairn, for He's a guid Shepherd for the feckless."

But now of a sudden a thought seemed to strike Henry, and he was on his feet in a twinkling and by my side.

"John," he almost screamed in my ear, "John, I'm going to ask ye for the greatest service that ever man asked. Ye'll no' say me nay?"

"Let me hear it," said I.

"Will *you* bide wi' the lass? You're a man o' birth, and, I'll swear to it, a man o' honour. I can trust you as I would trust my ain brither. O man, dinna deny me. It's the last hope I ha'e, for if ye refuse, we maun e'en gang to the hills and leave the puir thing alane. O ye canna say me nae. Tell me that ye'll do my asking."

I was so thunderstruck at the request that I scarce could

think for some minutes. Consider, was it not a strange thing to be asked to stay alone in a wild moorland house with another man's betrothed, for Heaven knew how many weary days? My life and prospects were none so cheerful for me to despise anything, nor so varied that I might pick and choose; but yet 'twas dreary, if no worse, to look forward to any length of time in this desolate place. I was grateful for the house as a shelter by the way, yet I hoped to push on and get rid, as soon as might be, of this accursed land.

But was I not bound by all the ties of gratitude to grant my host's request? They had found me fainting at their door, they had taken me in, and treated me to their best; I was bound in common honour to do something to requite their kindness. And let me add, though not often a man subject to any feelings of compassion, whatever natural bent I had this way having been spoiled in the wars, I nevertheless could not refrain from pitying the distress of that strong man before me. I felt tenderly towards him, more so than I had felt to anyone for many a day.

All these thoughts raced through my head in the short time while Master Henry stood before me. The look in his eyes, the pained face of the old man, and the sight of Anne so fair and helpless, fixed my determination.

"I am bound to you in gratitude," said I, "and I would seek to repay you. I will bide in the house, if so you will, and be the maid's protector. God grant I may be faithful to my trust, and may He send a speedy end to your exile!"

So 'twas all finished in a few minutes, and I was fairly embarked upon the queerest enterprise of my life. For myself I sat dazed and meditative; as for the minister and Master Semple, one half of the burden seemed to be lifted from their minds. I was amazed at the trusting natures of these men, who had habited all their day with honest folk till they conceived all to be as worthy as themselves. I felt, I will own, a certain shrinking from the responsibility of the task; but the Rubicon had been crossed and there was no retreat.

Of the rest of that night how shall I tell? There was such a bustling and pother as I had never seen in any house since the day that my brother Denis left Rohaine for the Dutch wars. There was a running and scurrying about, a packing of food, a seeking of clothes, for the fugitives must be off before the first light. Anne went about with a pale, tearful face; and 'twas a matter of no surprise, for to see a father, a man frail and fallen in years, going out to the chill moorlands in the early autumn till no man knew when, is a grievous thing for a young maid. Her lover was scarce in so dire a case, for he was young and strong, and well used to the life of the hills. For him there was hope; for the old man but a shadow. My heart grew as bitter as gall at the thought of the villains who brought it about.

How shall I tell of the morning, when the faint light was flushing the limits of the sky, and the first call of a heath-bird broke the silence! 'Twas sad to see these twain with their bundles (the younger carrying the elder's share) creep through the heather toward the hills. They affected a cheerful resolution, assumed to comfort Anne's fears and sorrow; but I could mark beneath it a settled despair. The old man prayed at the threshold, and clasped his daughter many times, kissing her and giving her his blessing. The younger, shaken with great sobs, bade a still more tender farewell, and then started off abruptly to hide his grief. Anne and I from the door watched their figures disappear over the crest of the ridge, and then went in, sober and full of angry counsels.

The soldiers came about an hour before mid-day—a

band from Clachlands, disorderly ruffians, commanded by a mealy-faced captain. They were a scurrilous set, their faces bloated with debauchery and their clothes in no very decent order. As one might have expected, they were mightily incensed at finding their bird flown, and fell to cursing each other with great good-will. They poked their low-bred faces into every nook in the house and outbuildings; and when at length they had satisfied themselves that there was no hope from that quarter, they had all the folk of the dwelling out on the green and questioned them one by one. The two serving-lasses were staunch, and stoutly denied all knowledge of their master's whereabouts—which was indeed no more than the truth. One of the two, Jean Crichope by name, when threatened with ill-treatment if she did not speak, replied valiantly that she would twist the neck of the first scoundrelly soldier who dared to lay finger on her. This I doubt not she could have performed, for she was a very daughter of Anak.

As for Anne and myself, we answered according to our agreement. They were very curious to know my errand there and my name and birth; and when I bade them keep their scurvy tongues from defiling a gentleman's house, they were none so well pleased. I am not a vain man, and I do not set down the thing I am going to relate as at all redounding to my credit; I merely tell it as an incident in my tale.

The captain at last grew angry. He saw that the law was powerless to touch us, and that nought remained for him but to ride to the hills in pursuit of the fugitives. This he seemed to look upon as a hardship, being a man to all appearance more fond of the bottle and pasty than a hill gallop. At any rate he grew wroth, and addressed to Anne a speech so full of gross rudeness that I felt it my duty to interfere.

"Look you here, sir," said I, "I am here, in the first place, to see that no scoundrel maltreats this lady. I would ask you, therefore, to be more civil in your talk or to get down and meet me in fair fight. These gentlemen," and I made a mocking bow to his company, "will, I am assured, see an honest encounter."

The man flushed under his coarse skin. His reputation was at stake. There was no other course open but to take up my challenge.

"You, you bastard Frenchman," he cried, "would you dare to insult a captain of the king's dragoons? I' faith, I will teach you better manners"; and he came at me with his sword in a great heat. The soldiers crowded round like children to see a cock-fight.

In an instant we crossed swords and fell to; I with the sun in my eyes and on the lower ground. The combat was not of long duration. In a trice I found that he was a mere child in my hands, a barbarian who used his sword like a quarter-staff, not even putting strength into his thrusts.

"Enough!" I cried; "this is mere fooling"; and with a movement which any babe in arms might have checked, twirled his blade from his hands and sent it spinning over the grass. "Follow your sword, and learn two things before you come back—civility to maids and the rudiments of sword-play. Bah! Begone with you!"

Some one of his men laughed, and I think they were secretly glad at their tyrant's discomfiture. No more need be said. He picked up his weapon and rode away, vowing vengeance upon me and swearing at every trooper behind him. I cared not a straw for him, for despite his bravado I knew that the fear of death was in his cowardly heart, and that we should be troubled no more by his visitations.

VI.

IDLE DAYS.

I HAVE heard it said by wise folk in France that the autumn is of all seasons of the year the most trying to the health of a soldier; since, for one accustomed to the heat of action and the fire and fury of swift encounter, the decay of summer, the moist, rotting air, and the first chill preludes of winter are hard to stand. This may be true of our own autumn days, but in the north country 'twas otherwise. For there the weather was as sharp and clear as spring, and the only signs of the season were the red leaves and the brown desolate moors. Lindean was built on the slope of the hills, with the steeps behind it, and a vista of level land to the front; so one could watch from the window the red woods of the low country, and see the stream, turgid with past rains, tearing through the meadows. The sun rose in the morning in a blaze of gold and crimson; the days were temperately warm, the afternoons bright, and the evening another procession of colours. 'Twas all so beautiful that I found it hard to keep my thoughts at all on the wanderers in the hills and to think of the house as under a dark shadow.

And if 'twas hard to do this, 'twas still harder to look upon Anne as a mourning daughter. For the first few days she had been pale and silent, going about her household duties as was her wont, speaking rarely, and then but to call me to meals. But now the pain of the departure seemed to have gone, and though still quiet as ever, there was no

melancholy in her air; but with a certain cheerful gravity
she passed in and out in my sight. At first I had had many
plans to console her; judge then of my delight to find them
needless. She was a brave maid, I thought, and little like the
common, who could see the folly of sighing, and set herself
to hope and work as best she could.

The days passed easily enough for me, for I could take
Saladin and ride through the countryside, keeping always
far from Clachlands; or the books in the house would stand
me in good stead for entertainment. With the evenings
'twas different. When the lamp was lit, and the fire burned,
'twas hard to find some method to make the hours go by.

I am not a man easily moved, as I have said; and yet I
took shame to myself to think of the minister and Master
Henry in the cold bogs, and Anne and myself before a great
blaze. Again and again I could have kicked the logs off to
ease my conscience, and was only held back by respect for
the girl. But, of a surety, if she had but given me the word, I
would have been content to sit in a fireless room and enjoy
the approval of my heart.

She played no chess; indeed, I do not believe there was
a board in the house; nor was there any other sport where-
with to beguile the long evenings. Reading she cared little
for, and but for her embroidery work I know not what she
would have set her hand to. So, as she worked with her
threads I tried to enliven the time with some account of
my adventures in past days, and some of the old gallant
tales with which I was familiar. She heard me gladly, listening as no comrade by the tavern-board ever listened; and
though, for the sake of decency, I was obliged to leave out
many of the more diverting, yet I flatter myself I won her
interest and made the time less dreary. I ranged over all
my own experience and the memory of those tales which
I had heard from others—and those who know anything

of me know that that is not small. I told her of exploits in
the Indies and Spain, in Germany and the Low Countries,
and in far Muscovy, and 'twas no little pleasure to see her
eager eyes dance and sparkle at a jest or grow sad at a sorrowful episode. *Ma vie!* She had wonderful eyes—the most
wonderful I have ever seen. They were gray in the morning and brown at noonday, now sparkling, but for the most
part fixedly grave and serene. 'Twas for such eyes, I fancy,
that men have done all the temerarious deeds concerning
womankind which history records.

It must not be supposed that our life was a lively one,
or aught approaching gaiety. The talking fell mostly to my
lot, for she had a great habit of silence, acquired from her
lonely dwelling-place. Yet I moved her more than once to
talk about herself.

I heard of her mother, a distant cousin of Master Semple's
father; of her death when Anne was but a child of seven;
and of the solitary years since, spent in study under her father's direction, in household work, or in acts of mercy to
the poor. She spoke of her father often, and always in such
a way that I could judge of a great affection between them.
Of her lover I never heard, and, now that I think the matter
over, 'twas no more than fitting. Once, indeed, I stumbled
upon his name by chance in the course of talk, but as she
blushed and started, I vowed to fight shy of it ever after.

As we knew well before, no message from the hills could
be sent, since the moors were watched as closely as the gate-
way of a prison. This added to the unpleasantness of the
position of each of us. In Anne's case there was the harass-
ing doubt about the safety of her kinsfolk, that sickening
anxiety which saps the courage even of strong men. Also,
it rendered my duties ten times harder. For, had there been
any communication between the father or the lover and the
maid, I should have felt less like a St Anthony in the desert.

As it was, I had to fight with a terrible sense of responsibility and unlimited power for evil, and God knows how hard that is for any Christian to strive with. 'Twould have been no very hard thing to shut myself in a room, or bide outside all day, and never utter a word to Anne save only the most necessary; but I was touched by the girl's loneliness and sorrows, and, moreover, I conceived it to be a strange way of executing a duty, to flee from it altogether. I was there to watch over her, and I swore by the Holy Mother to keep the very letter of my oath.

And so the days dragged by till September was all but gone. I have always loved the sky and the vicissitudes of weather, and to this hour the impression of these autumn evenings is clear fixed on my mind. Strangely enough for that north country, they were not cold, but mild, with a sort of acrid mildness; a late summer, with the rigours of winter underlying, like a silken glove over a steel gauntlet.

One such afternoon I remember when Anne sat busy at some needlework on the low bench by the door, and I came and joined her. She had wonderful grace of body, and 'twas a pleasure to watch every movement of her arm as she stitched. I sat silently regarding the landscape, the woods streaking the bare fields, the thin outline of hills beyond, the smoke rising from Clachlands' chimneys, and above all, the sun firing the great pool in the river, and flaming among clouds in the west. Something of the spirit of the place seemed to have entered into the girl, for she laid aside her needlework after a while and gazed with brimming eyes on the scene. So we sat, feasting our eyes on the picture, each thinking strange thoughts, I doubt not. By-and-by she spoke.

"Is France, that you love so well, more beautiful than this, M. de Rohaine?" she asked timidly.

"Ay, more beautiful, but not like this; no, not like this."

"And what is it like? I have never seen any place other than this."

"Oh, how shall I tell of it?" I cried. "'Tis more fair than words. We have no rough hills like these, nor torrents like the Lin there; but there is a great broad stream by Rohaine, as smooth as a mill-pond, where you can row in the evenings, and hear the lads and lasses singing love songs. Then there are great quiet meadows, where the kine browse, where the air is so still that one can sleep at a thought. There are woods, too—ah! such woods—stretching up hill, and down dale, as green as Spring can make them, with long avenues where men may ride; and, perhaps, at the heart of all, some old chateau, all hung with vines and creepers, where the peaches ripen on the walls and the fountain plashes all the summer's day. Bah! I can hardly bear to think on it, 'tis so dear and homelike"; and I turned away suddenly, for I felt my voice catch in my throat.

"What hills are yonder?" I asked abruptly, to hide my feelings.

Anne looked up.

"The hills beyond the little green ridge you mean," she says. "That will be over by Eskdalemuir and the top of the Ettrick Water. I have heard my father speak often of them, for they say that many of the godly find shelter there."

"Many of the godly!"

I turned round sharply, though what there was in the phrase to cause wonder I cannot see. She spoke but as she had heard the men of her house speak; yet the words fell strangely on my ears, for by a curious process of thinking I had already begun to separate the girl from the rest of the folk in the place, and look on her as something nearer in sympathy to myself. Faugh! that is not the way to put it. I mean that she had listened so much to my tales that I had all but come to look upon her as a countrywoman of mine.

"Are you dull here, Anne?" I asked, for I had come to use the familiar name, and she in turn would sometimes call me Jean—and very prettily it sat on her tongue. "Do you never wish to go elsewhere and see the world?"

"Nay," she said. "I had scarce thought about the world at all. 'Tis a place I have little to do with, and I am content to dwell here for ever, if it be God's will. But I should love to see your France, that you speak of."

This seemed truly a desire for gratifying which there was little chance; so I changed the subject of our converse, and asked her if she ever sang.

"Ay, I have learned to sing two or three songs, old ballads of the countryside, for though my father like it little, Henry takes a pleasure in hearing them. I will sing you one if you wish it." And when I bade her do so, she laid down her work, which she had taken up again, and broke into a curious plaintive melody. I cannot describe it. 'Twould be as easy to describe the singing of the wind in the tree-tops. It minded me, I cannot tell how, of a mountain burn, falling into pools and rippling over little shoals of gravel. Now 'twas full and strong, and now 'twas so eerie and wild that it was more like a curlew's note than any human thing. The story was about a knight who sailed to Norway on some king's errand and never returned, and of his lady who waited long days at home, weeping for him who should never come back to her. I did not understand it fully, for 'twas in an old patois of the country, but I could feel its beauty. When she had finished the tears stood in my eyes, and I thought of the friends I had left, whom I might see no more.

But when I looked at her, to my amazement, there was no sign of feeling in her face.

"'Tis a song I have sung often," she said, "but I do not like it. 'Tis no better than the ringing of a bell at a funeral."

"Then," said I, wishing to make her cheerful, "I will sing

you a gay song of my own country. The folk dance to it on the Sunday nights at Rohaine, when blind René plays the fiddle." So I broke into the "May song," with its lilting refrain.

Anne listened intently, her face full of pleasure, and at the second verse she began to beat the tune with her foot. She, poor thing, had never danced, had never felt the ecstasy of motion; but since all mankind is alike in nature, her blood stirred at the tune. So I sang her another chanson, this time an old love-ballad, and then again a war-song. But by this time the darkness was growing around us, so we must needs re-enter the house; and as I followed I could hear her humming the choruses with a curious delight.

"So ho, Mistress Anne," thought I, "you are not the little country mouse that I had thought you, but as full of spirit as a caged hawk. Faith, the town would make a brave lass of you, were you but there!"

From this hour I may date the beginning of the better understanding—I might almost call it friendship—between the two of us. She had been bred among moorland solitudes, and her sole companions had been solemn praying folk; yet, to my wonder, I found in her a nature loving gaiety and mirth, songs and bright colours—a grace which her grave deportment did but the more set off. So she came soon to look at me with a kindly face, doing little acts of kindness every now and then in some way or other, which I took to be the return which she desired to make for my clumsy efforts to please her.

VII.

A DAUGHTER OF HERODIAS.

THE days at Lindean dragged past, and the last traces of summer began to disappear from the face of the hills. The bent grew browner, the trees more ragged, and the torrent below more turgid and boisterous. Yet no word came from the hills, and, sooth to tell, we almost ceased to look for it. 'Twas not that we had forgotten the minister and Master Semple in their hiding, for the thought of them was often at hand to sadden me, and Anne, I must suppose, had many anxious meditations; but our life at Lindean was so peaceful and removed from any hint of violence that danger did not come before our minds in terrible colours. When the rain beat at night on the window, and the wind howled round the house, then our hearts would smite us for living in comfort when our friends were suffering the furious weather. But when the glorious sun-lit morning had come, and we looked over the landscape, scarce free from the magic of dawn, then we counted it no hardship to be on the hills. And rain came so seldom during that time, and the sun so often, that the rigour of the hill-life did not appal us.

This may account for the way in which the exiles slipped from our memories for the greater part of the day. For myself I say nothing—'twas but natural; but from Anne I must confess that I expected a greater show of sorrow. To look at her you would say that she was burdened with an old grief, so serious was her face; but when she would talk, then you might see how little her heart was taken up with the troubles of her house and the care for her father and lover. The girl to me was a puzzle, which I gave up all attempting to solve. When I had first come to Lindean, lo! she was demure and full of filial affection, and tender to her lover. Now, when I expected to find her sorrowful and tearful at all times, I found her quiet indeed, but instinct with a passion for beauty and pleasure and all the joys of life. Yet ever and anon she would take a fit of solemnity, and muse with her chin poised on her hand; and I doubt not that at such times she was thinking of her father and her lover in their manifold perils.

One day the rain came again and made the turf plashy and sodden, and set the Lin roaring in his gorge. I had beguiled the morning by showing Anne the steps of dancing, and she had proved herself a ready pupil. To pleasure her I danced the sword-dance, which can only be done by those who have great dexterity of motion; and I think I may say that I acquitted myself well. The girl stood by in wonderment, looking at me with a pleasing mixture of surprise and delight. She had begun to look strangely at me of late. Every now and then when I lifted my head I would find her great eyes resting on me, and at my first glance she would withdraw them. They were strange eyes—a mingling of the fawn and the tiger.

As I have said, in a little time she had acquired some considerable skill, and moved as gracefully as though she had learned it from her childhood, while I whistled bars of an old dancing tune. She had a little maid who attended her— Eff she called her—and the girl stood by to watch while Anne did my bidding. Then when we were all wearied of the sport, I fell to thinking of some other ploy, and could find none. 'Twas as dull as ditch-water, till the child Eff, by a good chance, spoke of fishing. She could get her father's

rod and hooks, she said, for he never used them now; and I
might try my luck in the Lin Water. There were good trout
there, it seemed, and the choice time of taking them was in
the autumn floods.

Now I have ever been something of a fisherman, for
many an hour have I spent by the big fish-pond at Rohaine.
So I got the tackle of Eff s father—rude enough it was in
all conscience—and in the early afternoon I set out to the
sport. Below the house and beyond the wood the Lin foams
in a deep gully, falling over horrid cascades into great churn-
ing pools or diving beneath the narrow rocks. But above the
ravine there is a sudden change. The stream flows equably
through a flat moor in sedgy deeps and bright shimmering
streams. Thither I purposed to go, for I am no lover of the
awesome black caldrons, which call to a man's mind visions
of drowned bodies and pits which have no ending. On the
moor with the wind blowing about one 'twas a pleasure to
be, but faugh! no multitude of fish was worth an hour in
that dismal chasm.

I had not great success, and little wonder, for my lei-
surely ways were ill suited for the alert mountain fish. My
time was spent in meditating on many things, but most of
all on the strange case in which I found myself. For in truth
my position was an odd one as ever man was in.

Here was I bound by my word of honour to bide in the
house and protect its inmates till that indefinite time when
its master might return. There was no fear of money, for
the minister had come of a good stock, and had more gear
than is usual with one of his class. But 'twas an evil thing
to look forward to—to spend my days in a lonely manse,
and wait the end of a persecution which showed no signs
of ending.

But the mere discomfort was nothing had it not been for
two delicate scruples which came to torment me. *Imprimis*,

'twas more than any man of honour could do to dwell in warmth and plenty, while his entertainers were languishing for lack of food or shivering with cold in the hags and holes of the mountains. I am a man tolerably hardened by war and travel, yet I could never abide to lie in bed on a stormy night or to eat my food of a sharp morning when I thought of the old man dying, it might be, unsheltered and forlorn. *Item*, there was the matter of the girl; and I cannot tell how heavy the task had come to lie on my shoulders. I had taken the trust of one whom I thought to be a staid country lass, and lo! I had found her as full of human passion as any lady of the court. 'Twas like some groom who offers to break a horse, and finds it too stiff in temper. I had striven to do my duty toward her and make her life less wearisome, and I had succeeded all too well. For I marked that in the days just past she had come to regard me with eyes too kindly by half. When I caught her unawares, and saw the curious look on her face, I could have bitten my tongue out with regret, for I saw the chasm to whose brink I had led her. I will take my oath there was no thought of guile in the maid, for she was as innocent as a child; but 'tis such who are oftentimes the very devil, since their inexperience adds an edge to their folly.

Thinking such thoughts, I fished up the Lin Water till the afternoon was all but past, and the sunset began to glimmer in the bog-pools. My mind was a whirl of emotions, and no plan or order could I conceive. But, and this one thing I have often marked, that the weather curiously affected my temper—the soft evening light brought with it a calm which eased me in the conflict. 'Tis hard to wrangle in spirit when the west is a flare of crimson, and each blue hill stands out sharp against the yellow sky. My way led through the great pine wood above the Lin gorge, thence over a short spit of heath to the hill path and the ordered shrubbery of the manse. 'Twas fine to see the tree stems stand out red against the gathering darkness, while their thick evergreen heads were blazing like flambeaus. A startled owl drove past, wavering among the trunks. The air was so still that the light and colour seemed all but audible, and indeed the distant rumble of the falling stream seemed the interpretation to the ears of the vision which the eyes beheld. I love such sights, and 'tis rarely enough that we see them in France, for it takes a stormy upland country to show to its full the sinking of the sun. The heath with its dead heather, when I came on it, seemed alight, as happens in March, so I have heard, when the shepherds burn the mountain grass. But in the manse garden was the choicest sight, for there the fading light seemed drawn to a point and blazing on the low bushes and coarse lawns. Each window in the house glowed like a jewel, but—mark the wonder—when I gazed over the country there was no view to be seen, but only a slowly-creeping darkness.

'Twas an eerie sight, and beautiful beyond telling. It awed me, and yet filled me with a great desire to see it to the full. So I did not enter the house, but turned my steps round by the back to gain the higher ground, for the manse was built on a slope. I loitered past the side window, and gained the place I had chosen; but I did not bide long, for soon the show was gone, and only a chill autumn dusk left behind. So I made to enter the house, when I noticed a light as of firelight dancing in the back window. Now I had never been in that room before, so what must I do in my idle curiosity but go peeping there.

The room was wide and unfurnished, with a fire blazing on the hearth. But what held me amazed were the figures on the floor. Anne, with her skirts kilted, stood erect and agile as if about to dance. The girl Eff sat by the fireplace, humming some light measure. The ruddy light bathed the floor and walls and made all distinct as noonday.

'Twas as I had guessed. In a trice her feet began to move, and soon she was in the middle of the first dance I had taught her, while *la petite* Eff sang the tune in her clear, low voice. I have seen many dancers, great ladies and country dames, village lasses and burgher wives, gipsies and wantons, but, by my honour, I never saw one dance like Anne. Her body moved as if by one impulse with her feet. Now she would bend like a willow, and now whirl like the leaves of the wood in an autumn gale. She was dressed, as was her wont, in sober brown, but sackcloth could not have concealed the grace of her form. The firelight danced and leaped in her hair, for her face was turned from me; and 'twas fine to see the snow of her neck islanded among the waves of brown tresses. With a sudden, swift dart she turned her face to the window, and had I not been well screened by the shadows, I fear I should have been observed. But such a sight as her face I never hope to see again. The solemnity was gone, and 'twas all radiant with youth and life. Her eyes shone like twin stars, the even brown of her cheeks was flushed with firelight, and her throat and bosom heaved with the excitement of the dance. Then she stopped exhausted, smiled on Eff, who sat like a cinder-witch all the while, and smoothed the hair from her brow.

"Have I done it well?" she asked.

"As weel as he did it himsel'," the child answered. "Eh, but you twae would make a bonny pair."

I turned away abruptly and crept back to the garden path, my heart sinking within me, and a feeling of guilt in my soul. I was angry at myself for eavesdropping, angry and ashamed. But a great dread came on me as I thought of the girl, this firebrand, who had been trusted to my keeping. Lackaday for the peace of mind of a man who has to see to a maid who could dance in this fashion, with her father and lover in the cold hills! And always I called to mind that I had

been her teacher, and that my lessons, begun as a harmless
sport to pass the time, were like to breed an overmastering
passion. *Mon Dieu!* I was like the man in the Eastern tale
who had raised a spirit which he was powerless to control.

And just then, as if to point my meditations, I heard the
cry of a plover from the moor behind, and a plaff of the
chill night-wind blew in my face.

VIII.

HOW I SET THE SIGNAL.

WHEN I set out to write this history in the English tongue, that none of my own house might read it, I did not know the hard task that lay before me. For if I were writing it in my own language, I could tell the niceties of my feelings in a way which is impossible for me in any other. And, indeed, to make my conduct intelligible, I should forthwith fall to telling each shade of motive and impulse which came to harass my mind. But I am little skilled in this work, so I must needs recount only the landmarks of my life, or I should never reach the end.

I slept ill that night, and at earliest daylight was awake and dressing. The full gravity of the case was open to me now, and you may guess that my mind was no easy one. I went down to the sitting-room, where the remains of the last night's supper still lay on the table. The white morning light made all things clear and obtrusive, and I remember wishing that the lamp was lit again and the shutters closed. But in a trice all meditations were cast to the winds, for I heard the door at the back of the house flung violently open and the sound of a man's feet on the kitchen floor.

I knew that I was the only one awake in the house, so with much haste I passed out of the room to ascertain who the visitor might be. In the centre of the back room stood a great swart man, shaking the rain from his clothes and hair, and waiting like one about to give some message. When he saw me he took a step forward, scanned me closely, and then waited my question.

"Who in the devil's name are you?" I asked angrily, for I was half amazed and half startled by his sudden advent.

"In the Lord's name I am Andrew Gibb," he responded solemnly.

"And what's your errand?" I asked further.

"Bide a wee and you'll hear. You'll be the foreigner whae stops at the manse the noo?"

"Go on," I said shortly.

"Thae twae sants, Maister Lambert and Maister Semple, 'ill ha'e made some kind o' covenant wi' you? At ony rate, hear my news and dae your best. Their hidy-hole at the heid o' the Stark Water's been betrayed, and unless they get warning it'll be little ye'll hear mair o' them. I've aye been their freend, so I cam here to do my pairt by them."

"Are you one of the hill-men?"

"Na, na! God forbid! I'm a douce, quiet-leevin' man, and I'd see the Kirk rummle aboot their lugs ere I'd stir my shanks frae my ain fireside. But I'm behauden to the minister for the life o' my bairn, whilk is ower lang a story for ye to hear; and to help him I would rin frae Maidenkirk to Berwick. So I've aye made it my wark to pick up ony word o' scaith that was comin' to him, and that's why I'm here the day. Ye've heard my news richt, ye're shure?"

"I've heard your news. Will you take any food before you leave?"

"Na; I maun be off to be back in time for the kye."

"Well, good-day to you, Andrew Gibb," I said, and in a minute the man was gone.

Now here I must tell what I omitted to tell in a former place—that when the exiles took to the hills they bade me, if I heard any word of danger to their hiding-place, to go by a certain path which they pointed out to a certain place, and there overturn a little cairn of stones. This was to be a signal to them for instant movement. I knew nothing of the place of their retreat, and for this reason could swear on my oath with an easy conscience; but this scrap of enlightenment I had, a scrap of momentous import for both life and death.

I turned back to the parlour in a fine confusion of mind. By some means or other the task which was now before me had come to seem singularly disagreeable. The thought of my entertainers—I am ashamed to write it—was a bitter thought. I had acquired a reasonless dislike to them. What cause had they, I asked, to be crouching in hill-caves and first getting honest gentlemen into delicate and difficult positions, and then troubling them with dangerous errands. Then there was the constant vision of the maid to vex me. This was the sorest point of all. For, though I blush to own it, the sight of her was not altogether unpleasing to me; nay, to put it positively, I had come almost to feel an affection for her. She was so white and red and golden, all light and gravity, with the shape of a princess, the mien of a goddess, and, for all I knew, the heart of a dancing-girl. She carried with her the air of comfort and gaiety, and the very thought of her made me shrink from the dark moors and ill-boding errand as from the leprosy.

There is in every man a latent will, apart altogether from that which he uses in common life, which is apt at times to assert itself when he least expects it. Such was my honour, for lo! I found myself compelled by an inexorable force to set about the performance of my duty. I take no credit for it, since I was only half willing, my grosser inclination being all against it. But something bade me do it, calling me poltroon, coward, traitor, if I refused; so ere I left the kitchen I had come to a fixed decision.

To my wonder, at the staircase foot I met Anne, dressed,

but with her hair all in disorder. I stood booted and cloaked and equipped for the journey, and at the sight of me her face filled with surprise.

"Where away so early, John?" says she.

"Where away so early, Mistress Anne?" said I.

"Ah, I slept ill, and came down to get the morning air." I noted that her eyes were dull and restless, and I do believe that the poor maid had had a sorry night of it. A sharp fear at my heart told me the cause.

"Anne," I said suddenly, "I am going on a hard errand, and I entreat you to keep out of harm's way till I return."

"And what is your errand, pray?" she asked.

"Nothing less than to save the lives of your father and your lover. I have had word from a secret source of a great danger which overhangs them, and by God's help I would remove it."

At my word a light, half angry and half pathetic, came to her eyes. It passed like a sungleam, and in its place was left an expression of cold distaste.

"Then God prosper you," she said in a formal tone, and with a whisk of her skirts she was gone.

I strode out into the open with my heart the battlefield of a myriad contending passions.

I reached the hill, overturned the cairn, and set out on my homeward way, hardly giving one thought to the purport of my errand or the two fugitives whom it was my mission to save, so filled was my mind with my own trouble. The road home was long and arduous; and more, I had to creep often like an adder lest I should be spied and traced by some chance dragoon. The weather was dull and cold, and a slight snow, the first token of winter, sprinkled the moor. The heather was wet, the long rushes dripped and shivered, and in the little trenches the peat-water lay black as ink. A smell of damp hung over all things, an odour of rotten leaves and soaked earth. The heavy mist rolled in volumes close to the ground and choked me as I bent low. Every little while I stumbled into a bog, and foully bedaubed my clothes. I think that I must have strayed a little from the straight path, for I took near twice as long to return as to go. A swollen stream delayed me, for I had to traverse its bank for a mile ere I could cross.

In truth, I cannot put down on paper my full loathing of the place. I had hated the moors on my first day's journey, but now I hated them with a tenfold hatred. For each whiff of sodden air, each spit of chill rain brought back to my mind all the difficulty of my present state. Then I had always the vision of Anne sitting at home by the fire, warm, clean, and dainty, the very counter of the foul morasses in which I laboured, and where the men I had striven to rescue were thought to lie hidden. My loathing was so great that I could scarce find it in my heart to travel the weary miles to the manse, every step being taken solely on the fear of remaining behind. To make it worse, there would come to vex me old airs of France, airs of childhood, and my adventurous youth, fraught for me with memories of gay nights and brave friends. I own that I could have wept to think of them and find myself all the while in this inhospitable desert.

'Twould be near mid-day, I think, when I came to the manse door, glad that my journey was ended. Anne let me in, and in a moment all was changed. The fire crackled in the room, and the light danced on the great volumes on the shelves. The grey winter was shut out and a tranquil summer reigned within. Anne, like a Lent lily, so fair was she, sat sewing by the hearth.

"You are returned," she said, coldly.

"I am returned," I said severely, for her callousness to the danger of her father was awful to witness, though in my

heart of hearts I could not have wished it otherwise. As she
sat there, with her white arms moving athwart her lap, and
her hair tossed over her shoulders, I could have clasped her
to my heart. Nay, I had almost done so, had I not gripped
my chair, and sat with pale face and dazed eyes till the fit
had passed. I have told you ere now how my feelings to-
ward Anne had changed from interest to something not unlike a passionate love. It had been a thing of secret growth,
and I scarcely knew it, till I found myself in the midst of it.
I tried to smother it hourly, when my better nature was in
the ascendant, and hourly I was overthrown in the contest.
I fought against terrible odds. 'Twas not hard to see from
her longing eyes and timorous conduct that to her I was the
greater half of the world. I had but to call to her and she
would come. And yet—God knows how I stifled that cry.

At length I rose and strode out into the garden to cool
my burning head. The sleet was even grateful to me, and
I bared my brow till hair and skin were wet with the rain.
Down by the rows of birch trees I walked, past the rough
ground where the pot-herbs were grown, till I came to the
shady green lawn. Up and down it I passed, striving hard
with my honour and my love, fighting that battle which all
must fight sometime or other in their lives and be victori-
ous or vanquished for ever.

Suddenly to my wonder I saw a face looking at me from
beneath a tuft of elder-berry.

I drew back, looked again, and at the second glance I
recognised it. 'Twas the face of Master Henry Semple of
Clachlands—and the Hills.

'Twas liker the face of a wild goat than a man. The thin
features stood out so strongly that all the rest seemed to
fall back from them. The long, ragged growth of hair on
lip and chin, and the dirt on his cheeks, made him unlike
my friend of the past. But the memorable change was in

his eyes, which glowed large and lustrous, with the whites greatly extended, and all tinged with a yellow hue. Fear and privation had done their work, and before me stood their finished product.

"Good Heavens, Henry, what brings you here, and how have you fared?"

He stared at me without replying, which I noted as curious.

"Where is Anne?" he asked huskily.

"She is in the house, well and unscathed. Shall I call her to you?"

"Nay, for God's sake, nay. I am no pretty sight for a young maid. You say she is well?"

"Ay, very well. But how is the minister?"

"Alas, he is all but gone. The chill has entered his bones, and even now he may be passing. The child will soon be an orphan."

"And you?"

"Oh, I am no worse than the others on whom the Lord's hand is laid. There is a ringing in my head and a pain at my heart, but I am still hale and fit to testify to the truth. O man, 'twill ill befa' those in the day of judgment who eat the bread of idleness, and dwell in peace in thae weary times."

"Come into the house; or nay, I will fetch you food and clothing."

"Nay, bring nought for me. I would rather live in rags and sup on a crust than be habited in purple and fare sumptuously. I ask ye but one thing: let the maid walk in the garden that I may see her. And, O man, I thank ye for your kindness to me and mine. I pray the Lord ilka night to think on ye here."

I could not trust myself to speak. "I will do as you wish," I said, and without another word set off sharply for the house.

I entered the sitting-room wearily and flung myself on a chair. Anne sat sewing as before. She started as I entered, and I saw the colour rise to her cheeks and brow.

"You are pale, my dear," I said; "the day is none so bad, and 'twould do you no ill to walk round the garden to the gate. I have just been there, and, would you believe it, the grass is still wondrous green."

She rose as demurely and obediently as if my word were the law of her life.

"Pray bring me a sprig of ivy from the gate-side," I cried after her, laughing, "to show me that you have been there."

I sat and kicked my heels till her return in a miserable state of impatience. I could not have refused to let the man see his own betrothed, but God only knew what desperate act he might do. He might spring out and clasp her in his arms; she, I knew, had not a shred of affection left for him; she would be cold and resentful; he would suspect, and then—what an end there might be to it all! I longed to hear the sound of her returning footsteps.

She came in soon, and sat down in her wonted chair by the fire.

"There's your ivy, John," said she; "'tis raw and chilly in the garden, and I love the fireside better."

"'Tis well," I thought, "she has not seen Master Semple." Now I could not suffer him to depart without meeting him again, partly out of pity for the man partly to assure my own mind that no harm would come of it. So I feigned an errand and went out.

I found him, as I guessed, still in the elder-bush, a tenfold stranger sight than before. His eyes burned uncannily. His thin cheeks seemed almost transparent with the tension of the bones, and he chewed his lips unceasingly. At the sight of me he came out and stood before me, as wild a figure as I

ever hope to see—clothes in tatters, hair unkempt, and skin
all foul with the dirt of the moors. His back was bowed, and
his knees seemed to have lost all strength, for they tottered
against one another. I prayed that his sufferings might not
have turned him mad.

At the first word he spake I was convinced of it.

"I have seen her, I have seen her!" he cried. "She is more
fair than a fountain of gardens, a well of living waters, and
streams from Lebanon. Oh, I have dreamed of her by night
among the hills, and seen her face close to me and tried to
catch it, but 'twas gone. O, man John, get down on your
knees, and pray to God to make you worthy to have the
charge of such a treasure. Had the Lord not foreordained
that she should be mine, I should ne'er have lifted up my
eyes to her, for who am I?"

"For God's sake, man," I broke in, "tell me where you
are going, and be about it quick, for you may be in instant
danger."

"Ay," says he, "you are right. I must be gone. I have
seen enough. I maun away to the deserts and caves of the
rocks, and it may be lang, lang ere I come back. But my
love winna forget me. Na, na; the Lord hath appointed unto
me that I shall sit at His right hand on the last, the great
day, and she shall be by my side. For oh, she is the only
one of her mother; she is the choice one of her that bare
her; the daughters saw her and blessed her; yea, the queens
and concubines, and they praised her." And with some like
gibberish from the Scriptures he disappeared through the
bushes, and next minute I saw him running along the moor
towards the hills.

These were no love-sick ravings, but the wild cries of
a madman, one whose reason had gone for ever. I walked
back slowly to the house. It seemed almost profane to think
of Anne, so wholesome and sane, in the same thought as

this foul idiot; and yet this man had been once as whole in mind and body as myself; he had suffered in a valiant cause; and I was bound to him by the strongest of all bonds—my plighted word. I groaned inwardly as I shut the house-door behind me and entered into the arena of my struggles.

IX.

I COMMUNE WITH MYSELF

Twas late afternoon when I re-entered, and ere supper was past 'twas time to retire for the night. The tension of these hours I still looked back on as something altogether dreadful. Anne was quiet and gentle, unconscious of what had happened, yet with the fire of passion, I knew too well, burning in her heart. I was ill, restless and abrupt, scarce able to speak lest I should betray my thoughts and show the war that raged in my breast.

I made some excuse for retiring early, bidding her goodnight with as nonchalant an air as I could muster. The door of my bedroom I locked behind me, and I was alone in the darkened room to fight out my battles with myself.

I ask you if you can conceive any gentleman and man of honour in a more hazardous case. Whenever I tried to think on it, a mist came over my brain, and I could get little but unmeaning fantasies. I must either go or stay. So much was clear.

If I stayed—well, 'twas the Devil's own work that was cut for me. There was no sign of the violence of the persecution abating. It might be many months, nay years, before the minister and Master Semple might return. If they came back no more, and I had sure tidings of their death, then indeed I might marry Anne. But 'twas so hazardous an uncertainty that I rejected it at once. No man could dwell with one whom he loved heart and soul so long a time on such uncertain chances and yet keep his honour. Had the maid been dull and passive, or had I been sluggish in blood, then there might have been hope. But we were both quick as the summer's lightning.

If they came back, was not the fate of the girl more hard than words could tell? The minister in all likelihood would already have gone the way of all the earth; and she, poor lass, would be left to the care of a madman for whom she had no spark of liking. I pictured her melancholy future. Her pure body subject to the embraces of a loathsome fanatic, her delicate love of the joys of life all subdued to his harsh creed. O God! I swore that I could not endure it. Her face, so rounded and lovely, would grow pinched and white, her eyes would lose all their lustre, her hair would not cluster lovingly about her neck, her lithe grace would be gone, her footsteps would be heavy and sad. He would rave his unmeaning gibberish in her ears, would ill-treat her, it might be; in any case would be a perpetual sorrow to her heart. "O Anne," I cried, "though I be damned for it, I will save you from this."

If I left the place at once and forever, then indeed my honour would be kept, but yet not all; for my plighted word—where would it be? I had sworn that come what may I should stand by the maid and protect her against what evil might come to the house. Now I was thinking of fleeing from my post like a coward, and all because the girl's eyes were too bright for my weak resolution. When her lover returned, if he ever came, what story would she have to tell? This, without a doubt—"The man whom you left has gone, fled like a thief in the night, for what reason I know not." For though I knew well that she would divine the real cause of my action, I could not suppose that she would tell it, for thereby she would cast grave suspicion upon herself. So there would I be, a perjured traitor, a false friend in the eyes of those who had trusted me.

But more, the times were violent, Clachlands and its soldiery were not far off, and once they learned that the girl was unprotected no man knew what evil might follow. You may imagine how bitter this thought was to me, the thought of leaving my love in the midst of terrible dangers. Nay, more; a selfish consideration weighed not a little with me. The winter had all but come; the storms of this black land I dreaded like one born and bred in the South; I knew nothing of my future course; I was poor, bare, and friendless. The manse was a haven of shelter. Without it I should be even as the two exiles in the hills. The cold was hard to endure; I dearly loved warmth and comfort; the moors were as fearful to me as the deserts of Muscovy.

One course remained. Anne had money; this much I knew. She loved me, and would obey my will in all things; of this I was certain. What hindered me to take her to France, the land of mirth and all pleasant things, and leave the North and its wild folk behind for ever? With money we could travel expeditiously. Once in my own land perchance I might find some way to repair my fortunes, for a fair wife is a wondrous incentive. There beneath soft skies, in the mellow sunshine, among a cheerful people, she would find the life which she loved best. What deterred me? Nothing but a meaningless vow and some antiquated scruples. But I would be really keeping my word, I reasoned casuistically with myself, for I had sworn to take care of Anne, and what way so good as to take her to my own land where she would be far from the reach of fanatic or dragoon? And this was my serious thought, *comprenez bien!* I set it down as a sign of the state to which I had come, that I was convinced by my own quibbling. I pictured to myself what I should do. I would find her at breakfast in the morning. "Anne," I would say, "I love you dearly; may I think that you love me likewise?" I could fancy her eager, passionate reply, and

then——I almost felt the breath of her kisses on my cheek
and the touch of her soft arms on my neck.

Some impulse led me to open the casement and look
forth into the windy, inscrutable night. A thin rain distilled
on the earth, and the coolness was refreshing to my hot
face. The garden was black, and the bushes were marked
by an increased depth of darkness. But on the grass to the
left I saw a long shaft of light, the reflection from some
lit window of the house. I passed rapidly in thought over
the various rooms there, and with a start came to an end.
Without a doubt 'twas Anne's sleeping-room. What did the
lass with a light, for 'twas near midnight? I did not hesitate
about the cause, and 'twas one which inflamed my love an
hundredfold. She was sleepless, love-sick maybe (such is the
vanity of man). Maybe even now my name was the one on
her lips, and my image the foremost in her mind. My finger-
tips tingled, as the blood surged into them; and I am not
ashamed to say that my eyes were not tearless. Could I ever
leave my love for some tawdry honour? *Mille tonneres;* the
thing was not to be dreamed of. I blamed myself for having
once admitted the thought.

My decision was taken, and, as was always my way, I felt
somewhat easier. I was weary, so I cast myself down upon
the bed without undressing, and fell into a profound sleep.

How long I slept I cannot tell, but in that brief period
of unconsciousness I seemed to be living ages. I saw my
past life all inverted as 'twere; for my first sight was the
horror of the moors, Quentin Kennedy, and the quarrel,
and the black desolation which I had undergone. I went
through it all again, vividly, acutely. Then it passed, and I
had my manhood in France before my eyes. And curiously
enough, 'twas not alone, but confused with my childhood
and youth. I was an experienced man of the world, versed
in warfare and love, taverns and brawls, and yet not one

whit jaded, but fresh and hopeful and boylike. 'Twas a very pleasing feeling. I was master of myself. I had all my self-respect. I was a man of unblemished honour, undoubted valour. Then by an odd trick of memory all kinds of associations became linked with it. The old sights and sounds of Rohaine: cocks crowing in the morning; the smell of hay and almond-blossom, roses and summer lilies; the sight of green leaves, of the fish leaping in the river; the plash of the boat's oars among the water-weeds—all the sensations of childhood came back with extraordinary clarity. I heard my mother's grave, tender speech bidding us children back from play, or soothing one when he hurt himself. I could almost believe that my father's strong voice was ringing in my ear, when he would tell stories of the chase and battle, or sing ballads of long ago, or bid us go to the devil if we pleased, but go like gentlemen. 'Twas a piece of sound philosophy, and often had it been before me in Paris, when I shrank from nothing save where my honour as a gentleman was threatened. In that dream the old saying came on me with curious force. I felt it to be a fine motto for life, and I was exulting in my heart that 'twas mine, and that I had never stained the fair fame of my house.

Suddenly, with a start I seemed to wake to the consciousness that 'twas mine no more. Still dreaming, I was aware that I had deceived a lover, and stolen his mistress and made her my bride. I have never felt such acute anguish as I did in that sleep when the thought came upon me. I felt nothing more of pride. All things had left me. My self-respect was gone like a ragged cloak. All the old, dear life was shut out from me by a huge barrier. Comfortable, rich, loving, and beloved, I was yet in the very jaws of Hell. I felt myself biting out my tongue in my despair. My brain was on fire with sheer and awful regret. I cursed the day when I had been tempted and fallen.

And then, even while I dreamed, another sight came to

my eyes—the face of a lady, young, noble, with eyes like
the Blessed Mother. In my youth I had laid my life at the
feet of a girl, and I was in hopes of making her my wife.
But Cecilia was too fair for this earth, and I scarcely dared
to look upon her she seemed so saint-like. When she died
in the Forest of Arnay, killed by a fall from her horse, 'twas
I who carried her to her home, and since that day her face
was never far distant from my memory. I cherished the image as my dearest possession, and oftentimes when I would
have embarked upon some madness I refrained, fearing the
reproof of those grave eyes. But now this was all gone. My
earthy passion had driven out my old love; all memories
were rapt from me save that of the sordid present.

The very violence of my feeling awoke me, and I found
myself sitting up in bed with a mouthful of blood. Sure
enough, I had gnawed my tongue till a red froth was over
my lips. My heart was beating like a windmill in a high gale,
and a deadly sickness of mind oppressed me. 'Twas some
minutes before I could think; and then—oh joy! the relief! I
had not yet taken the step irremediable. The revulsion, the
sudden ecstasy drove in a trice my former resolution into
thinnest air.

I looked out of the window. 'Twas dawn, misty and wet.
Thank God, I was still in the land of the living, still free to
make my life. The tangible room, half lit by morning, gave
me a promise of reality after the pageant of the dream. My
path was clear before me, clear and straight as an arrow;
and yet, even now I felt a dread of my passion overcoming
my resolve, and was in a great haste to have done with it
all. My scruples about my course were all gone. I would
be breaking my oath, 'twas true, in leaving the maid, but
keeping it in the better way. The thought of the dangers
to which she would be exposed stabbed me like a dart. It

had almost overcome me. "But honour is more than life or love," I said, as I set my teeth with stern purpose.

Yet, though all my soul was steeled into resolution, there was no ray of hope in my heart—nothing but a dead, bleak outlook, a land of moors and rain, an empty purse and an aimless journey.

I had come to the house a beggar scarce two months before. I must now go as I had come, not free and careless as then, but bursting shackles of triple brass. My old ragged garments, which I had discarded on the day after my arrival, lay on a chair, neatly folded by Anne's deft hand. It behoved me to take no more away than that which I had brought, so I must needs clothe myself in these poor remnants of finery, thin and mud-stained, and filled with many rents.

X.

OF MY DEPARTURE.

I PASSED through the kitchen out to the stable, mark-
ing as I went that the breakfast was ready laid in the
sitting-room. There I saddled Saladin, grown sleek by fat
living, and rolling his great eyes at me wonderingly. I tested
the joinings, buckled the girth tight, and led him round to
the front of the house, where I tethered him to a tree and
entered the door.

A savoury smell of hot meats came from the room and
a bright wood fire drove away the grayness of the morning.
Anne stood by the table, slicing a loaf and looking ever and
anon to the entrance. Her face was pale as if with sleep-
lessness and weeping. Her hair was not so daintily arranged
as was her wont. It seemed almost as if she had augured the
future. A strange catch—coming as such songs do from no-
where and meaning nothing—ran constantly in my head.
'Twas one of Philippe Desportes', that very song which the
Duke de Guise sang just before his death. So, as I entered, I
found myself humming half unwittingly:—

> "Nous verrons, bergère Rosette,
>   Qui premier s'en repentira."

Anne looked up as if startled at my coming, and when
she saw my dress glanced fearfully at my face. It must have
told her some tale, for a red flush mounted to her brow and
abode there.

I picked up a loaf from the table. 'Twas my one sacrifice

to the gods of hospitality. 'Twould serve, I thought, for the first stage in my journey.

Anne looked up at me with a kind of confused wonder. She laughed, but there was little mirth in her laugher.

"Why, what would you do with the loaf?" said she. "Do you seek to visit the widows and fatherless in their affliction?"

"Nay," said I gravely. "I would but keep myself unspotted from the world."

All merriment died out of her face.

"And what would you do?" she stammered.

"The time has come for me to leave, Mistress Anne. My horse is saddled at the door. I have been here long enough; ay, and too long. I thank you with all my heart for your kindness, and I would seek to repay it by ridding you of my company."

I fear I spoke harshly, but 'twas to hide my emotion, which bade fair to overpower me and ruin all.

"Oh, and why will you go?" she cried.

"Farewell, Anne," I said, looking at her fixedly, and I saw that she divined the reason.

I turned on my heel, and went out from the room.

"O my love," she cried passionately, "stay with me; stay, oh, stay!"

Her voice rang in my ear with honeyed sweetness, like that of the Sirens to Ulysses of old.

"Stay!" she cried, as I flung open the house door.

I turned me round for one last look at her whom I loved better than life. She stood at the entrance to the room, with her arms outstretched and her white bosom heaving. Her eyes were filled with an unutterable longing, which a man may see but once in his life—and well for him if he never sees it. Her lips were parted as if to call me back once more. But no word came; her presence was more powerful than any cry.

I turned to the weather. A gray sky, a driving mist, and a chill piercing blast. The contrast was almost more than my resolution. An irresistible impulse seized me to fly to her arms, to enter the bright room again with her, and sell myself body and soul to the lady of my heart.

My foot trembled to the step backward, my arms all but felt her weight, when that blind Fate which orders the ways of men intervened. Against my inclination and desire, bitterly, unwillingly, I strode to my horse and flung myself on his back. I dared not look behind, but struck spurs into Saladin and rode out among the trees.

A fierce north wind met me in the teeth, and piercing through my tatters, sent a shiver to my very heart.

THE END.

Afterword: The alternative ending to *Sir Quixote*

The alternative, American, ending of *Sir Quixote*, which appeared in the first American edition of the novel published by Henry Holt and Company, New York, in 1895, is problematic. It consists of two sentences added to the "British" ending.

> I cannot recall my thoughts during that ride: I seem not to have thought at all. All I know is that in about an hour there came into my mind, as from a voice, the words: "Recreant! Fool!" and I turned back.

As can be seen, these few words change the sense of the last third of the book, since they mean that de Rohaine has changed his mind one more time, and has returned to claim Anne for his own.

What are we to make of such an alteration? By changing his mind yet again de Rohaine has demonstrated agonising uncertainty over the choice between the two extremes of natural affection and the dictates of honour. By changing his mind for a final time, the agonising has made his behaviour that of a weather-cock, of a ditherer. This does not fit well with his earlier constancy and reliability in the book, but might be read as a reminder of his loose and apparently dissolute character: in fact, the kind of behaviour that drove him to take what a later century would call a "repairing lease" in times of temporary financial difficulties. There is also the matter that returning for Anne would have been a betrayal of the memory of de Rohaine's former love, the dead Cecilia, which had such a powerful effect on him earlier in the novel. The "happy" ending could be read as a subtextual revelation that de Rohaine is not reliable, and may not be a happy match for Anne, intimating tragedy a little further down the line. Buchan was probably right to send de Rohaine away.

According to David Daniell, the British scholar who has written most on the novel, the first American edition of the novel, which contained this alternative ending, was "pirated."[1] In 1981

the standard bibliography of Buchan's works by Robert Blanchard
noted that the American edition's addition to the end of the novel
"was apparently done at the request of the American publishers
in order to imply a 'happy' ending of the story."[2] While the archives of Henry Holt and Company have still to be examined for
correspondence on this matter, it is unlikely that any survives
concerning this exceedingly obscure publication in the early
years of the firm's existence.[3] It has to be said that American publishers frequently "pirated" British novels without permission in
this period, since the copyright laws at that time permitted them
to do so as long as no other American publisher was deprived of
sales of the same title.[4] Holt may have bagged *Sir Quixote* after its
publication in London by T. Fisher Unwin, and Buchan may have
had no say in the matter. He may not even have known for some
time that an American edition had appeared at all.

The existence of the extra ending begs the question of who
wrote it, and why. If Buchan's novel had been taken by Holt to
publish for profit without needing to pay royalties to the author,
then the happy ending must have been supplied by Holt's firm,
since Buchan would not have written something extra for no return. If Buchan had known and sanctioned the American edition,
would he have written such an ending? A "happy" ending would
indeed have had a better chance of selling, turning *Sir Quixote*
into a standard novelette of the period. The American reader
would have been presented with period romance in fancy dress,
rather than the stark and rather tortured ending that Buchan had
originally devised.

This can be seen as a symptom of the clash between the
emerging modernistic trend in new fiction of the *fin de siècle*,
particularly in Britain, which was challenging the dominance of
cheap sensational fiction, sold in vast quantities at a penny, in
Britain and the USA, and also published in cheap paperback for-
mats. Holt said himself, only twenty years later, that "we" (the
USA) "publish few books as compared with other civilised nations, but we issue more periodicals than all other nations put
together. We publish 60% of the periodical literature, so to call it,
of the world."[5] Buchan may have collaborated with his American

publishers, by providing the alternative ending to manipulate a different market sector. It is more likely that the publishers took the "property" and gave it the new ending to make it more saleable, and ignored what the author might have thought, had he even known about it. However, Buchan's refusal to allow the novel to be reprinted in 1918 may be a reflection of the shabby treatment his work received on its first appearance.

NOTES

1   David Daniell, *The Interpreter's House. A Critical Assessment of the Work of John Buchan*. London: Nelson, 70.
2   Robert Blanchard, *The First Editions of John Buchan. A Collector's Bibliography*. Hamden, Conn.: Archon Books, 1981, 5.
3   The Henry Holt & Co. Archives are apparently held at the Firestone Library at Princeton University (Gilbert 9). The author would be glad to hear about any correspondence between Holt and Buchan concerning *Sir Quixote*.
4   Gilbert, Ellen D., *Henry Holt & Co., 1866-1946. An Editorial History*. Unpublished Ph.D. thesis, Columbia University, 1992.
5   Henry Holt, "American Literature is Going to the Dogs," *New York Times*, 9 January 1916.

GLOSSARY

a'	all
ails	to be upset, afflicted
ain	own
airt	way, road
alane	alone
Anak	a tall and strong person (Numbers 13:33)
aneath	beneath
auld	old
bairn	child
baith	both
befa'	befall, take place
behauden	beholden, indebted to
bide	stay
bide a wee	wait a moment
bielded	sheltered
bit	little
black-avised	dark features, swarthy appearance
bonny	beautiful
brave	fine-looking
brawly	richly
brawling	fast, active
brither	brother
choler	anger
coorse	coarse
coursing	hunting deer
dae	do
dirlin'	to shake violently ; to dangle
douce	sedate, quiet, careful
een	eyes
e'en	even, thus
Embro'	Edinburgh
ethert	adder, type of snake
flambeaus	torches

frae	from
forbye	indeed
freend	friend
fremt	strange, unfamiliar, foreign
gang	go
gaun	going
gear	household goods
gey, gey-like	very
guid	good
ha'e	have
haugh	flat ground near a river bank
heather-busses	heather-bushes
heid	head
hunkering	crouching
ilka	every
jalouse	guess, assume
ken	know
kye	cows
lang	long
leevin'	living
licht	light
lugs	ears
mair	more
maun	must
mony	many
moss-hags	ridges of peat-bog
muckle	much
nae	no
nicht	night
noo	now
ony	any
oot	out
out-bye	outside
ower	over
pairt	part
pastern	the horse's leg between fetlock and hoof
plaff	gust

puir	poor
to redd	to tidy up, to smarten up
reive	to steal, to plunder
rig	ridge
rin	run
Rubicon	the point beyond which there can be no turning back
rummle	to shake, to jostle
sants	saints
scaith	harm
sic	such
shanks	legs
swart	dark, heavy
syne	since
thegither	together
thole	endure
toots	(minor exclamation of exasperation)
tush	(minor exclamation of deprecation)
twain	two
wae	reluctant
wark	work
warstle	wrestle
waur	worse
weary	bad, terrrible
whae	who
whilk	which
win to	reach
winna	will not
yin	one